Dalton

THE MCCADE DRAGON BOOK 4

KATHI S. BARTON

World Castle Publishing, LLC
Pensacola, Florida
Copyright © Kathi S. Barton 2017
Paperback ISBN: 9781629897295
eBook ISBN: 9781629897301
First Edition World Castle Publishing, LLC, June 26, 2017
http://www.worldcastlepublishing.com

Licensing Notes

Cover: Karen Fuller
Editor: Maxine Bringenberg

Chapter 1

There were no words that he could say that would make this any different. Dalton watched as the casket, a beautiful bright wood, was lowered into the cold earth. His friend, mentor, and sounding board had died eight days ago. Howard Short simply went to sleep one night and didn't wake. And it broke Dalton's heart.

"Dalton?" He looked at Melinda, Howard's wife, when she said his name. "Will you say a few words, please? My brother-in-law just can't. He's devastated, as we all are."

"Yes, of course." He stood up and made his way to the podium. So many people were here today, paying tribute to a wonderful man. Dalton thought of his friend and what he could say about him. Smiling, he remembered something that Howard would have gotten a kick out of. "Howard could be a jackass when he wanted."

Everyone laughed, just as he'd hoped, even Melinda. He continued speaking about Howard as if he'd just stepped out for a cold beer.

"When we were on a stakeout or even out fishing, he'd tell me of the time he was in the academy. Of course, I didn't believe half the crap he told me. But this one story, I think, sums him up better than anything I could say about him." Dalton looked at the casket, then at the people there. "He'd been in the dorm for about two weeks, he'd told me. It wasn't going as well as he'd hoped. I think he said that of the three classes he was in, he was flunking out of three of them."

Another round of laughter. "Back then, if you weren't cutting it, Howard told me that they'd come to see you, help you pack up your things, and send you on your way. He wasn't ready to give up, he told me, and he didn't think that they should be just yet either.

"As he was debating on whether or not to open the door when his time came, he had an idea. Howard told me it wasn't a good idea, but he'd been down and was sure under other circumstances, he might not have done what he did next. He opened the door and told the men standing there that Howard Short had left.

"Left, they asked him, and Howard said he told him that the old Howard had decided that he wasn't smart enough for this shit and that he wanted him, the new Howard, to try his hand at it. They asked him if he was new or old. Howard assured him that he was the new one." Dalton thought of the man that he'd become that day. "The new Howard was given a chance. He was either going to straighten up his act, they told him, or new or not, he was going home. Howard assured them that he'd be a better man and the best cop they'd ever had graduate out of that place."

Dalton nodded as he continued the story told to him so many times, he felt as if he had been there with the man. "He not only became the best cop they'd ever had come from that place, but he continued to be the best person who ever lived. Howard ran a tight but friendly ship, he took care of his men when they needed a helping hand, and he was there for them, even when they didn't want him to be, when things were going to shit. Howard was, and will forever be, the best friend I've ever had."

After he was finished, he stood still as the guns were drawn for the salute and fired. Dalton cried then, his pain of loss too much for him to hold in any longer. And when the service was over, he made his way to Melinda again and hugged her. She too had become a very important part of his life over the years.

"You'll come to visit me, won't you?" He told her he would. She was leaving today, to live with her son in another state. "He loved you so much, Dalton. Like his own son."

"I loved him as well. He'll be sorely missed."

She nodded and left him there. Dalton could have gone to stand with his family, but decided that he was fine where he was. He watched as the dirt was filled into the hole much like the one in his heart. But his would never be filled.

Going to the after reception at the newly remodeled homeless shelter, he didn't speak to many people. There was food, he supposed, that he could have eaten, but like his heart, his belly wasn't ready for anything right at the moment. Instead he just found a dark corner and sat in it until he felt it was a good time for him to go home.

My lord. He wanted to sob. Dalton didn't want to answer who he thought was talking to him. It could only mean one thing, and he didn't want it. Not today, perhaps not ever. *My lord, your mate is coming.*

"Tell her that I've got a lot going on at the moment and I'd prefer that she didn't." Caelin said nothing. "Where is she and what does she have?"

The hair combs, my lord. And I don't think it's possible for her not to come. She is on her way now. But I must tell you that she hasn't put the jewelry to her flesh. I'm not at all sure why just yet, but she is aware of me and is coming this way. He asked what the combs did for the wearer. *She will have blood that will heal all that she touches, her heart will be stronger still than it was before.*

Her name is —

"No, don't tell me. I mean, I know that I'll have to know sooner or later, but for now I'd like to just not know." Caelin told him he could do that for him. "Has she been hurt in any way? Are there beings even now trying to kill her?"

Nay, she is well. Healthy, if not a bit overworked. I think she will be more inclined to not believe the story as to why she needs to come here than even Emma was. And she is not a pushover. He asked him how he knew that. *Whilst I was speaking with her, to see if she was injured or harmed in any way, I felt her anger. Before I could comment on it, or even ask her what happened, she had an argument with her boss that...I think she said it curled his toes back.*

Dalton laughed. "She's a hellion, then. Good, she'll need to be to fit in with this group. I don't suppose you know just when she'll arrive, do you? I mean, I have a lot of things going on at the moment."

She has arrived. This morning, as a matter of fact. But as I have said, she is not wearing the jewels. You will need to have her put them to her in order for me to help her should she need me. Dalton figured it would be something like that. *She has asked to join your brother, Kenton, in his practice. She is not yet aware that she is with the very people that are to help her. I don't believe he has given her an answer as yet.*

"She's a nurse then?" Caelin told him she was a doctor. "A doctor? Well that's great, don't you think? Once I'm out of work, she can support me."

You are without a job, sir? He told him that he might well be. *I don't understand. I thought you enjoyed being a good cop. Whatever has...? Is it the death of your captain?*

"He was my sergeant, but yes, because of him passing away, I don't think my heart will be in this anymore. I might... never mind. If she can support me, I think I might just make furniture in my garage until I turn up dead one morning. Or

I'll run off and never return."

Dalton realized then that she was out of work too. They were starting off great, he thought. Two unemployed people with a huge house, no car, and nothing to show for their hard work. When Vance sat down beside him, he asked him when he'd gotten in.

"Two days ago. I've been working on some things." Dalton nodded. "Rumor has it you're the next big cheese around here. You gonna be sheriff now, Dalt?"

Vance had been the only person who called him that. It mattered little to him that Dalton had asked him not to call him Dalt…he had continued over the years.

Dalton asked him where he'd heard that rumor. "Because that's all it is, a rumor. I'm not going to take the job. In fact, I was seriously thinking of quitting altogether." Vance told him that he'd not enjoy retirement any more than he would. "Caelin just told me that my mate is here in town."

"Really? I'm assuming that it's the pretty little doctor at the B&B then?" Dalton didn't want to ask about her, but found he wanted to know. "Yes, she is pretty. Tall…though not quite as tall as you, but close. Blonde hair that I assume is long. Dark eyes. I've not seen them as yet close up, but I'd say they were blue, like midnight blue."

"You know a great deal about my mate, Vance. What have you been doing, spying on her?" He nodded. "Whatever for? You think she's some sort of murderer or something? It wouldn't surprise me. Not at this point."

"No, but she has baggage." Dalton just stared at him. "Her job, where she worked before, they really have a hard-on for her to come back to work for them. I don't believe they have it in their head to kidnap her or such, but they have been trying to find her."

"What did she do? I mean, she didn't just leave them high

9

and dry, did she?" He said that she'd given her notice, but that they'd not looked for a replacement thinking they could change her mind. "I see. Well, not really. Was she that good or did they take advantage of her?"

"Both, I think. She is highly regarded as a physician. Much like Kenton is in his profession. She does have some surgical abilities, and from what I've heard, she can also put in stitches better than anyone around. These are things that patients have said about her." Dalton asked again why he was doing this. "To be honest with you, had you not told me she was your mate, I was going to try and set her up with Lewis. He's been...distracted lately."

That was an understatement. He was working hard at getting a restaurant opened or something. He was very secretive about it, but that's what Dalton thought he was doing. Not that he didn't have the funds to do it, but he had been getting deliveries out the ass for the last few days. Emma had offered to lend him what he needed in the way of funds—so had he and Kenton—but Lewis was determined to do this on his own, whatever that might be. He did wonder if he could go work for him for a bit, just to figure out what he wanted to do with the rest of his life.

"I guess I should just wait for her then. I mean, I don't want to seem like that odd stalker guy." Vance said he had no idea, but thought that was a smart move. He knew less about women than Dalton did, apparently. "Whatever you do, I'm sure that it'll be either wrong or not enough. I know nothing at all about women."

Dalton looked at his brother. He was clean but his pants were Army issue, his shirt a dark tee, and his boots—ass kickers, he called them—had seen better days. Vance kept his hair military short and neat, and he seldom had a beard. Dalton asked him why he didn't wear...well, regular people clothing.

"I wear what I want, when I want." Dalton laughed. "Look, whether you go and see her or not, you should know that she's polite, generous with her time, and like you, she wears what she does right out there for everyone to see." He asked him what that meant. "You are a cop, Dalt. Even a blind man could tell that. And they'd not even have to see the badge. Same with her. She's a doctor, a good one, and people know that when they first see her."

Dalton sat there long after Vance left, trying to figure out what to do. He could have, he supposed, just walked over to meet her, but he had a feeling that would have been a mistake. He was sure that he could talk to Kenton too, but decided that he'd get enough grief from him without adding to it. Instead, he went to his truck and drove home. Dalton was going to enjoy the next few days he had off, and not worry about mates, dragons, or men looking for jewelry.

~~~

Gabe walked to the diner. She'd come to love the little place with the strange way they served their meals and the nice people who worked in and frequented it. As she made her way inside, she knew which seat to sit in, which to avoid. When she sat in the booth with the unforgiving spring, she moved to the window, just so she'd not be sore when the sucker pinched her. Milly came to take her order.

"Breakfast?" Nodding, she held the cup as the hot water was poured into it, knowing the small basket of tea bags would follow soon. "Got us some specials today. Cook is feeling a little good. He's got himself a little boy now, and just don't know what to do with himself."

"Anything that I might wish to try?" Milly asked her how brave she was feeling. "Not too bad. Do I need to be?"

"Nah, you can handle it. He's got some sausage patty

11

sammiches, and he made up some kind of casserole with last night's taters. Got some cheese and stuff in it too. I liked it with a little gravy on it." Gabe wondered how much this woman considered a little. She had a heavy hand when it came to about anything. And the funny part of that was, she was as thin as a rail and looked to be fairly healthy, too. "I'll bring you a plate. I thought about calling it the blue plate, but we don't have any so that won't work."

Milly left her a second time after dropping off the basket with an assortment of teas in it. Gabe enjoyed her tea as she waited on her food, and thought about what her line up was for the rest of the day. She had an interview with Kenton McCade, and hopefully the house that she'd been looking at was ready to be rented. Things were going quite nicely for a change, and she was as rested and happy as she'd ever been.

"Oh lordy." Gabe looked up when she heard the shout from the kitchen, then Milly saying "Oh lordy" over and over. Getting up, she ticked off all the things that could go wrong in a kitchen, and was afraid that Milly had been hurt badly. As soon as she entered, she put her fingers in her mouth and let go of a shrill but effective whistle to shut the few people in the room up.

A dishwasher was wearing the nastiest apron she'd ever seen and dark gloves on his hands. Milly was standing there wringing her hands. A man, who she assumed was the cook, was lying on the floor with a large knife sticking out of his belly, his hands covered in his own blood and his eyes wide with terror. Gabe let her mind take over on what to do.

"Milly, call the police and have them send an ambulance." She'd learned the first day that there was no one manning the nine-one-one service just yet. "Then I want you to get everyone out of here while I fix this."

"The knife, it just slipped up." Gabe nodded and told her

12

she had it. "He's surely gonna bleed to death, and Kenton, he won't make it in time."

"I'm a doctor as well. I've got this. Just do what I told you." She made her way to Cook. If he had a name, she'd never heard it. "I'm Gabe. If you'll allow me, I'll see if I can help you."

"I think I'm a goner. The knife, it's stainless steel but it's in me." She told him as long as she was there, he wasn't. "I wasn't paying no attention to what I was doing. Thinking of my boy and what we was gonna do when he was a mite bigger. Now I won't see him."

He was getting weaker; the arm that was holding him up slipped out from under him and he fell back to the floor. Gabe got her first look at the wound. He'd cut his belly to his intestine, the knife still inside him.

Turning to the person who'd come in behind her when she'd entered, she told him to get some towels. When he didn't move, just stared at Cook with his mouth open, she tossed the pan at him that had been on the floor. That got him looking at her.

"Towels. Get me as many as you can carry. And water." He moved, and it was then that she realized he was just a kid. When he returned, a gallon of water in one hand and several towels in the other, she told him to go to the dining area.

"I can help." Gabe wasn't sure, the kid was green now. "My name is Gavin, and I can help you. Just tell me what to do, I'm okay now."

"We have to close this. Otherwise he's going to bleed out. But I have to make sure that he didn't open his bowel. Can you handle that?" He said that he'd try. "Good. When I tell you something, I want you to do it. And remember what I tell you. It will save his life."

They worked for ten minutes checking Cook's belly.

13

He'd nicked his lower bowel, she thought, but wasn't sure that removing the knife wouldn't do more damage. She told Gavin that.

"Uncle Kenton is on his way. He said for you to do what you needed to do and he'd assist when he gets here." She wasn't sure how that conversation had happened but said nothing to the young man. "I told him what I could."

"You can...You're not human." He told her he was, but Kenton wasn't. "I see. Right now I have more important things to do than to figure out what he might be. This is what we need to do. Christ, there is never a vampire around when you need one."

The laughter made her smile. It was one thing to scare the kid to death over something like this, but making him see humor wouldn't give him nightmares too. As she moved the towels around the blade, all she could think about was that he might be right...Cook might die.

When Kenton showed up, his black bag in hand, he asked her what he could do. It both surprised and impressed her that he didn't just come in and take over. For the next twenty minutes, he handed her what she wanted and helped her when necessary. The impromptu surgery room wasn't the best, but it was going to be good enough to save this man's life. The medics, a couple young men she assumed were friends of Kenton, stayed back until they were ready to transport him. It wasn't long after Kenton arrived that they were able to say they'd done the best that they could for the man. The rest was going to be up to the surgeon.

Gabe rode in the ambulance, Kenton beside her. The medic rode in front with the driver, so in the event that they needed to, they'd have room to work. As they worked together, she and Kenton, Cook came around once to tell Kenton to watch over his son for him.

"You're going to make it, Gerald." She nearly asked who that was when the cook nodded. "The good doctor here, she got you all put back together, and once we get you to the hospital, she's going to remove that knife and you'll be as good as new. But you have to believe us, Gerald. You know as well as I do that if you give up on her, Sandra is going to kick my ass. You hear me?"

"Yes, she's a mite mean when she wants to be." Gerald moved in and out of consciousness and talked to them both when he was awake. "Had I been able to, I'd of just shifted, but not with a knife in my gullet."

It had never occurred to her that the man wasn't human. Not that it mattered, but she might have removed the knife and let him shift. Kenton spoke to her in low tones as Gerald was out again.

"Had you removed the blade from him in the kitchen, he would have been too weak to shift and he would have died. You did right by waiting." She told him what she'd been thinking. "I could see that on your face. Don't second guess yourself when you work for me. If you do, then you'll fuck up."

"Am I? Going to work for you, I mean?" He just grinned. It made him look more handsome, and she was pretty sure he used that a lot to his advantage a lot. "I'm having troubles from the hospital where I came from. They won't release my records."

"I don't need them. As far as I'm concerned, you proved yourself to be a worthy partner." She nodded and looked down at Gerald. "You said that he could have died had I removed the knife. I don't understand a great deal about shifters."

"You'll learn. Gerald is a wolf. There is a lot of pack around the area. Nearly seven hundred now. The people who

15

own the B&B where you're staying, they're bears. Milly is human, but she's married to a cat." She asked him what his family was. "My brother is a cop. He'll be meeting us at the hospital. He has to fill out a report for insurance purposes. Milly owns the place, and while she'd never tell anyone this, she's fallen on some hard times of late and can't afford this hit to her bank account."

"She needs to fix up the place. Expand a little, and for the love of all that is holy, get some better seating." Gabe didn't point out that he'd not answered her as to what he was. She figured that he either didn't want her to know, or it was so bad that he didn't want to share. "I'm looking for a house. One that is ready to move into. I don't want to have to fix something up."

"We have a few. We're here." Just as he said that, the ambulance made a hard stop. Had she not been holding on, she would have fallen out of the door when it opened. The man standing there in a police officer's shirt and jeans did not look happy. "Dalton, this is my new partner, Gabriela Nola. Gabe, this is Dalton McCade. We're dragons."

She was halfway out of the back of the ambulance when Kenton spoke. Gabe felt her breath swoosh out of her and her heart simply stop beating. She knew they were speaking, arguing really, but nothing was getting through. Not air, sound, nor even blood was running in her body. Then the pain, like someone had slapped her, registered a split second before the world around her just disappeared.

CHAPTER 2

Dalton was going to murder Kenton. The fucking bastard. He'd done that on purpose. As he carried the beautiful woman to the gurney, he thought of all the ways he was going to get back at his brother. First, he was going to have him ticketed every single time he came into town. Then she looked up at him.

"I've fallen." He told her she'd fainted. "No, I don't faint. I'm made of stronger stuff than a woman that swoons."

Dalton couldn't help it, he laughed. And, of course, that pissed her off more. Helping her to sit up afforded him the opportunity to touch her, and he did. When she started to stand as well, he halted her with his hand at her chest.

"You should rest a bit first. That was a big...tumble you took just now." The glare was wonderful, but Dalton was careful not to show her his reaction. "Kenton is in surgery with Gerald. He said all he was going to do was remove the knife, then stitch him up enough that he could regain his strength to shift."

"He said he was a dragon. Did that guy...Peterson, did he pay Kenton to tell me that? Because I have to tell you, I don't think it's the least bit funny." Dalton asked her what she meant. "A dragon. Kenton, he said that he was a dragon. I don't think that's funny."

17

"Kenton *is* a dragon. So am I." The glare again. "Perhaps it would help me if you just, for a moment, believed me and told me about this Peterson person."

"I was in my office. I'm not entirely sure how he got it, but he gave me this present. Well, he didn't, it was from this other guy, Waterson. I was there when his grandson was declared deceased." Dalton nodded and helped her to the chair. Not that she needed it, but it was just too much fun not to help her enough to piss her off. "Will you please let me go?"

"No, I don't think so. Waterson...you were telling me about his grandson and a present." He could tell she was really upset, and as much as he wanted to tell her it wasn't important, he thought that if she didn't tell him now, he'd never find out the story. "Did you open the present?"

"No, I didn't...this little boy had been killed. There was nothing I could have done for him by the time he was brought in. His father — he's in jail now — had shot him in the head. But Mr. Waterson had somehow.... Peterson said that Waterson had spoken to a dragon. A dragon that the dead child in my emergency room had warned me about a few days before. I'm not making any sense. Let me start again." And this time, the story that she told him was more coherent, less jumbled around.

"I'm sorry." She nodded and he lifted her chin up to look into her eyes. "This gift, why haven't you opened it? I mean, it was for you. The man wanted you to have it."

"I don't want it. Every time I even looked at the box, it would remind me of that child." Dalton could understand that. When she glanced at him, he could see her resignation, her fear too. "Are you really a dragon? I mean, it's okay if you are, but it would really go a long way to my sanity if you're not."

"I'm sorry. But yes, I'm a dragon." He got down on his

18

knees before her. "Tell me what's happened since you were told about us. Why did you come here? Did a voice tell you anything that you would like to share with me?"

"He never shuts up." Dalton laughed and said he knew that as well. "He never mentioned a name. He just said that I was to bring you this gift, whatever it was, and that it would bring me all that I'd ever want. I want a lot of things, Dalton... nothing extraordinary, just things to make my life less hectic."

"I'm almost afraid to tell you this, but I think your life just got more hectic, and the dragon won't shut up at all from now on either." Dalton straightened up and put out his hand. "I'd very much like for you to trust me right now. I know it's a lot to ask, but I'd like to have you listen to me with an open mind, all right?"

She nodded, but spoke before he could continue. "This is real, isn't it? I'm sitting here with a dragon about to take my hand, and I'm going to be so fucked, aren't I?"

He wanted to tell her she was going to be fucked. Dalton wasn't crude...he cursed less than his brothers did even though he was around men who did it like it was their job. But in this, he would gladly have strung a few of them together to show her just how frustrated he was about all this too. Instead, he just told her to trust him.

They made their way to the waiting room. Kenton assured Dalton that he was nearly done and asked that Gabe wait. He told her what his brother said and then spoke to her about things around the town. Mostly they chatted about the diner and Milly.

"Kenton said she was having some financial troubles. I was...I don't know Milly at all, but I was wondering if you thought she'd take an investor." Dalton asked her what she meant. "Well, I think if she just updated a few things, maybe hired more help, she'd be able to make a difference."

19

"But she'd have to pay an investor, right?" Gabe told him that it didn't always work that way. "Explain it to me, like you would Milly. You met her, right? She's a nice lady, and a great deal smarter than she lets out, but she loves that diner like it's her child."

"All right. I could.... No, that won't work. Let me think." Dalton loved the way her mind was working out the best way to approach this. He'd gone to Milly before, a while back, and had asked her to be a partner with him. But she'd turned him down flat. "She's not the type of person that having something written out on a graph and charts would help. She's more of a hands on, show me what you mean sort of person. I think that I'd just have to start small with her. Perhaps lend her the money to get one new seat."

"The one with the nasty spring." Gabe nodded and laughed. "Yeah, that one has gotten me a couple of times. Kenton had to stitch me up once when I got it in my thigh."

"Yes, well, you learn very quickly to move only when necessary when sitting there. But the chair and that table need to be replaced. I think it would only cost about five hundred to get both of them replaced. Unless you know someone that could repair it. That way it stays in the community." He liked that idea and told her so. "I've noticed that this town is making some headway into growing. There is no reason to buy out when it can be done here."

"The pack might have someone. In fact, I bet my mom would know. Just a few months ago she had her dining room chairs redone. I'll ask her. Then what would you do?"

They talked about changes, small ones that would help Milly. In all, it wasn't that much, but it would make great strides in getting her more business. Gabe pointed out that with the nicer seating and a new countertop on the dining end of the business, Milly could have at least twenty more seats opened up, thus making more room for someone to come in.

Kenton joined them with Gerald about thirty minutes later.

"Are you all right?" Instead of answering her, Gerald hugged her. Sobbing, he told Gabe how he'd thought he was a goner, and that he'd never see his son grow up. "You just have to be more careful next time. I might not be there having breakfast when you hurt yourself again."

"You'll come in every day. I'll serve you up the best for no charge." She told him that wasn't necessary. "It is to me. I owe you my life, and a wolf never forgets. Pack, they will see it the same way as I do, too."

When she started to protest again, Dalton reached for her hand and squeezed it. She looked at him but didn't object again. He had a feeling that she understood what he was trying to convey, and she hugged Gerald once more before he left. Kenton wanted them to come to his office to talk.

"I've just gotten off the phone with Mercy Hospital. They're saying that you have a contract with them until the end of the year." He watched Gabe reach into her purse and pull out a thick envelope. After handing it to Kenton, she sat back and waited. After his brother read it, he handed it to Dalton and leaned back. "You're a smart woman. Having this, you know that this means you can come straight to work here and have hospital privileges."

"Yes." Without reading the contents of the envelope, Dalton asked what it was she had done. "I came here about six months ago and registered as a physician. I filed what I needed in my state and with my job, and asked to be able to apply for a license to practice here. The hospital emailed me that form and I had my attorney go over it. He then came up with something that stated that they're willing to forgo the rest of my contract in the event that I take this test at my own

21

expense and didn't miss any work in doing so. That allowed me to take my boards here without a conflict of interest on my part."

"You covered your butt pretty good on this." She nodded and looked at Kenton, then back at him. "What is it?"

"I had no idea when I got all this taken care of that dragons would be involved. Not that I have anything against them. I don't care what you are so long as you don't hurt me. But this thing, this dragon, Caelin, he told me that there would be people chasing me for it. Trying to kill me for whatever is in that box. It's one of the other reasons that I've never opened it. He said that if I did, then there would be more."

"More?" She nodded at him. "You've encountered someone already? You've been chased? Hurt?"

Standing up, she lifted her blouse. The bruise was fresh, some of it still red in places and darkening in others. As he ran his fingers over it, not even sure why, she moaned and he looked into her eyes. Christ, his body was on fire. For her. Kenton cleared his throat.

"I'd like to have a look at that." The low sound that came from Dalton's lips startled him. Kenton too, if his face was any indication. "You can be in the room as well. I just want to make sure that there are no broken ribs and that we document this. There is no telling what someone might say later."

"I'm all right. Really. I don't even know that any of them, whoever they were, had anything to do with it. I haven't been harmed since this guy tried to take me out with his car. For all we know, it just might have been an accident." Kenton said he'd still like to make sure. "All right. But I want answers. I don't have a lot of questions that I can sort out at the moment, but I have some. If you would...I need a place to stay. A car. Things like that. The rest...well, I'll have to work on those, like I said."

"I think we can take care of most of that immediately. However, I think that you and Dalton need to talk." She looked at him and Dalton stood up. "It's about lunch time, so why don't you go home, talk, and I'll call you in the morning."

Kenton just left them there, closing the door softly behind him. Dalton wasn't sure what to do now, but he figured that talking was in order. But before he could do much more than suggest they go to his house, Gabe's phone rang.

~~~

"I don't know what to tell you." Her head was hurting. She was so stressed from the few moments that she'd been on the phone that she wanted to just sit down and bawl. Or throw the phone across the room and be done with it. "I told you already that I've given my notice. I took myself out of the rotation, off the schedule, and transferred any patients that I had over to the on-call service. I no longer work for you, and I have no obligations to you either."

"But we aren't making as much money as we were when you were here. Wilson wants overtime for his work. The college won't send us any more students because they claim that we're working them too much." Gabe said that they were. "They were free labor. What would you have done? Oh I know, you would have coddled them and given them whatever they wanted. Well, that's not the way to run a business."

"Perhaps not, but it's also considered bad form to kill your workforce simply because you're too cheap to give them a break." Gabe looked at the piece of paper Dalton handed her. In a way to talk to the man on the other end of the phone and answer Dalton, she said her former boss's name. "Look, Doctor Howe, I'm not an employee of your hospital any longer. I haven't been for nearly two months now. I would suggest that you open that tight money bag you have a hold

23

on and hire some good staff. A doctor that is willing to help you out, as well as more nurses. They're going to walk if you don't start easing up on them. As for me coming back there, that's not going to happen. Not ever, so you should really get that out of your little head right now."

"Are you threatening me, Gabriela?" She told him she didn't care enough about him to do so. "But you said the staff was going to walk. Are you telling me that they are planning it? If so, you can tell them for me that I will fire the lot of them if they try. I have a business to run, and I will not have my balls in a vise simply because you think you can just walk away from here and tell the staff to do the same."

"You see? That's your problem right there. You think just because you're in charge of the hospital that it's your own personal battleground. And that's what it is, Dr. Howe, a battleground. You have less than half the nurses you need to run the place. You've alienated the two local colleges so much that they have petitioned to not just have you removed as hospital administrator, but to have your charter to be a teaching hospital revoked. In about six months, less I'm betting, your hospital is going to close down because you're going to lose the college money."

"Who told you these things? Where are you getting your information? It's wrong, just so you know. We're doing just fine." He cleared his throat, and she could see him stretching his neck and letting out a long breath to cool off. "Now. We're going to be civilized about this, Gabriela. I would like to know why you've left us in a pickle, and what you're going to do to fix it. It's only fair that you come back here. We're the ones that gave you your first job."

"You did. But we both know that I could and should have done better. I'm not getting you out of your pickle, nor am I coming back there. I've got a good job. Take me off your calling list and do not contact me again, Dennis. I'm finished."

After disconnecting, she had to stand there for several minutes. When her fingers were peeled from the phone and it was taken from her, she sat down in the chair. Gabe felt tears fill her eyes as she thought of how good of an impression she must be making right now.

"I heard him." She nodded to Dalton. "He's a little prick, isn't he? And stupid if he thinks he's going to be able to get you to go back with that sort of incentive."

"I was working about ninety hours a week there. When they offered me a salary position about four years ago, I was supposed to get a cost of living raise with it every year. I did, but not without a fight. My brother-in-law, Jamie, he had to take them to court last year just to get half of what I should have gotten from them." He asked her about her sister. "Rachel. She passed away several years ago. Cancer. Jamie and I have been...I guess you could say we're closer than in-laws. Not sexually, but like brother and sister."

"It's always nice to have someone in your corner." She sat there, trying to get her temper under control when Dalton spoke again. "What do you know of mates?"

"Mates are what shifters call their other half. It's a good relationship for the most part. No harm rule, or something in their DNA. It doesn't always work that way, but most of the time. Mates don't stray, nor do they lie to each other. The children of mated couples grow up to be well adjusted, happy, and usually they're not troublemakers. But like most species, humans included, there is always that one bad apple that makes the rest of them look bad." She looked at him. "You have a reason for asking me?"

"Yes, you're my mate." She'd known he was going to say that, as surely as she was sitting there, and that next he was going to tell her that she was his to do with as he pleased.

25

She really didn't think he'd use her, not this guy, but it was just one more thing she'd have to deal with. "I'd like to know what you're thinking right now."

"No, you wouldn't." Dalton smiled and said that he really would. "I don't need any more crap in my life, Dalton. I'm dealing with enough, don't you think? I'm out of work...well, I was out of work. I have no home, no car, and a dragon that speaks to me all hours of the day and night. Men are chasing me for a box that I don't know what's in it. And now you tell me that you're my mate, like it's going to be a good thing. No, I don't need any more stress added at the moment."

"All right. A little unfair, but I can deal with that right now. Like you said, you're not out of a job. So you know, Kenton is the best there is when it comes to working with a person. He's a good man, and you'd not do any better than having him as a partner. House. I have one. And you can move into it and I'll go stay with my mom if you're uncomfortable sharing a home with me right now. She won't mind, and until we can figure this thing out between us, it might be best." Gabe asked him why. "Because as of the moment that I touched you and you moaned, all I can think about is stripping you down to your bare skin and tasting every morsel of you. The dragon has his own rules—he speaks to me as well—but I doubt that he would continue if you were to ask him to only do so to you when necessary, and during hours that—"

"Wait. Just wait a minute." Dalton grinned at her and she had the sudden urge to hit him. Hard and many times. "What do you mean, you want to...? You only just met me, and you want to have sex with me? That's not.... What if you...? I'm not even sure how to continue with you saying something like that. You cannot be serious."

He stood up and pulled her up as well. Before she could guess his intentions, he kissed her. It was hot, all consuming, and wonderfully fulfilling at the same time. Gabe grabbed him. Her purpose was to push him away, but he cupped her ass and pulled her to his cock. Then it was everything she could do not to have him lift her up and take her. Christ, the man was good at seduction was all her mind could think of.

His mouth was hot, wet, and his tongue was dancing with hers like he owned her. Right now she would have gladly relinquished anything she had to him if he would continue touching her the way he was. His hands were everywhere, his mouth doing things to her that had her wet, and her nipples hard. And when he lifted his head, she licked her lips to take more of his taste into her.

"Does this make you realize just how serious I am?" She nodded. "I would love to have all of you. Lay you out over Kenton's desk and feast on your pussy. Lap at you until you came down my throat. Would you enjoy that, Gabriela?"

"Yes." Even to her own ears she sounded breathless. And when Dalton let her go and stepped back from her, she wanted to cry. Or beg him. Then someone knocked on the door, and she had a feeling that Dalton knew who it was. When the door opened, she backed from it as the man there came into the room like he owned it.

"Vance, you're scaring her." The man stopped moving, but she had a feeling that in a second he'd be moving again. A man on a mission. Someone who got the job done.

He reminded her of steam engines and the power behind them. Of men that would come into her hospital and demand that she do things, make things happen to their client, her patient, that was both against the law and unethical. But when he looked at her, she saw something she was sure he hadn't meant for anyone to see.

The man was haunted.

"I was hoping Kenton was in here." Dalton said he'd just

left. "Okay. I'll come back later."

"No, let me see." She had no idea how she knew that he was hurt, and that it was far worse than he would have ever admitted to anyone but Kenton. And only then because he needed help. "Show me where you've been hurt and let me take care of it."

"I don't think that's a good idea." She told him to sit, and when he staggered to the table, she, with the help of Dalton, moved him. "I'm all right."

"Sure you are. And I'm positive that you think whatever happened was only a scratch. Stop being a pigheaded jackass and let me see." As soon as he was laying back on the table, she saw the blood. "What am I working with?"

"Gunshot wounds. A few of them. Loss of blood. Dizzy and sick." Nodding, she turned to Dalton and told him to get her a cart from the ER. "I don't need people knowing that I'm here and why. Lately I've been able to take care of it on my own, but I think I've not healed yet because there are just too many of them in me."

"Well, I guess it sucks to be you then. And when this is done, I want to know why you think.... You know what? I don't care." Gabe turned to Dalton. "Tell them that Kenton wants the cart to help interview me for the job. That it's a test or something. Just let them know that it's to be a full cart, no shorts. They'll know what that means."

As soon as he was gone, assuring her that he'd be right back, she looked at her patient. He had his eyes closed, but she'd bet her last dollar that he could tell her if there was a fly buzzing around the room and where it was. She told him to lie still.

"You're a bossy little thing, anyone ever tell you that before?" She told him plenty have. "Well, I don't care for it. Just so you know."

28

"Tough shit." She cut away his shirt when he handed her his knife. "Three GSW, one through and through. Second one more than likely broke a rib or two. The last needs to be removed."

He grabbed her arm when she touched him. It was painful, but she was pretty sure that he had no idea how hard he was holding her.

"No one, you understand. No one can know."

She nodded once, and grabbed him as he started to slide off the table. He had passed out. Whether from loss of blood or pain she had no idea, but she got to work as soon as Dalton returned.

CHAPTER 3

Vance woke up, but didn't move. It took him several seconds to figure out where he was and how the fuck he'd gotten there. He looked at the woman asleep in the chair across from him. Christ, she was a pretty little thing. Vance looked to his right when he felt another person in the room. Dalton nodded.

She's pretty pissed off at you at the moment. So am I, if you want to know the truth. He asked him what he'd done now. *You hit her. Slugged her hard enough to blacken her eye and cheek. If you hadn't already been down, I would have put you there myself.*

I'm sorry. He looked at her again, but the way she had her head tilted back, he couldn't see what he'd done. *I'm fucking sorry. Is she really pissed?*

Nah. She was at me. I tried to wrestle you away from her and she lit into me like Mom does when she's hot. Wow, what a temper. Vance rolled to his back, careful of the wounds. *You want to tell me why you were shot four times and wouldn't let us tell anyone?*

Four? No, three. Dalton said he'd counted them. *Okay, maybe it was four. I fucking don't know. I was running.*

Vance thought about not telling him anything. There were times, he knew, that they didn't know what he did for a living, but there were times when he wished he could unload on one of them, just for a little while. Or who he worked with.

31

Instead, he looked over at the doctor and then at his brother. If he was honest, Vance was lonely.

I was looking into some things at the warehouse down by the river. The one that no one seems to own but work is constantly going on there. You know which one I'm talking about? Dalton said he had men watching it. *I'd find new ones. If what I saw there this — I don't know the date, but the morning I came to see Kenton — they're helping unload a few trucks and store the shit in there.*

Two days ago. So they've been bought. Vance told him he thought it was more that they had something over them. Or someone. *You're saying that they're holding their family in order to get them to look the other way? Why? What did you find out?*

Contraband cigarettes. Not at all sexy, but it pays good money. I mean, even prostitution doesn't pay as well as a few thousand packs of cancer sticks. Dalton leaned back in the chair. He knew that this brother would understand that more than anyone. *I'd say without a doubt that there are more than seven thousand cartons of them going out of that place a week. If what I found out is right, then someone is collecting the taxes on that, because when they leave the warehouse, they're stamped.*

The government sent you in. Vance didn't even blink. *All right. No answer, I guess, is as good as one. So what is it you're doing about it? I'm assuming something.*

Yes. He couldn't tell Dalton the rest. That would get his brother killed. Because Dalton was a good man and a better cop. *If I asked you to stay out of it, would you?*

He glanced at Gabe, then at him, and nodded. *She's my mate, as you know. And I need her in my life. I can't have her going in all gung-ho if something happens to me. You either. I think she is going to make you do things you will not like when she wakes up.*

Like what? Before Dalton could answer him, Gabe sat up. Vance felt his heart twist in his chest when he saw how badly he'd injured her. "Christ, I am so very sorry. I didn't mean to

32

hurt you."

"You were in pain. It's fine." She stood up and went to him, and Vance ran his finger over her face. It was swollen and dark from his hand, and he sat up and told her again how sorry he was. "You think this is the first time a patient has hit me? It's not. I've been hit dozens of times. Broken ribs, a few fingers smashed up. I once had to have thirty-three stitches in my forehead when a kid no bigger than the one that helped me...Gavin...no bigger than him was high on something and thought I was trying to take his drugs. He used the barf basin that I had for him to beat me to shit, then a few days later he was killed. Nasty shit, drugs."

"But I wasn't high and I hurt my sister." When she looked at Dalton then at him again, Vance had an understanding. "You haven't talked, have you? He's your mate, love. And as of the moment that you two came together, you became family. My family, for better or worse."

"We have talked, but some macho ass came in and interrupted us. And speaking of which, I'd like to talk to you about the tracker you have in your leg." He frowned, not understanding her. "You have one. Let me show you."

He'd had his pants removed by someone and he didn't want to think it was her. Vance didn't want anyone to see his battered body, but especially not this woman. When she turned his leg so that he could see the long scar there, he told her how he'd gotten it.

"I was jumping a fence and I didn't quite make it over. It's old." She asked if she could show him the tracker. "How would you do that?"

"Cut you. I can numb it for you, though I don't think it's that deep. But it's there. I can.... I'm joking. I have an x-ray of it. When you were out, I had portable equipment brought in. Again, under the guise of training. Kenton had to be informed because of what I was doing with the equipment, and he saw it too. Not my fault in this...I had to have help as I'm not a doctor anyone would know as yet." She reached into the small drawer by the bed and pulled out a folder. "I didn't mean to snap you here, but I wasn't used to using the machine by myself, and I caught this image."

It was of his left leg. Gabe pointed to the long ago break in his fibula, as well as some small shrapnel in his calf, neither of which bothered him. But it was the small cylinder shaped thing that had his full attention.

"I could have removed it while you were out, but I had no idea if you had it put there or if it would go off or something if I did. I saw one like this once, when I was volunteering overseas. This kid had it." He asked her if she had a better picture. "Yes. If you want the numbers off it, you're going to have to give me something in return."

Vance wanted to lash out at her, but he held his tongue when Dalton stood up. He'd kill him if he attacked, and Vance loved his brother too much to fight him back if it came to just fists. Instead, he just stood up and towered over Gabe.

"What do you think I have to give you, Gabe? Money?" She shook her head. "Then what? What sort of demands will you make of me since you know something that I don't?"

"Don't be a fucking prick." Her tone and words shocked him. "Sit the fuck down and get your fucking panties out of a twist before I do it for you. You're all that and more, I can see that, but guess what, jackass? I don't want to fight you; I want to save you."

He'd just had his ass handed to him by a woman. Sitting down, he told her he was sorry again. When she sat down as well, he felt like the biggest jerk that had ever lived. Vance felt the last fifteen years of his career, his work, and his life hit him right in the heart.

"I'm sorry." She told him not to worry about it, but not to assume with her. "No, I won't, not again. What is it you want me to do?"

"That thing in your leg. You have any idea who could've done that?" He said was aware of maybe a couple. "I might be able to help you along with that. I have a buddy, he's.... Well, he won't care for you...he's not into the macho manly type. He's gay, and likes his men to be diminutive and a lot on the feminine side. He'll help me, but you have to play nicely with him or he won't help."

"What is it you think he can help me with, and why would he?" Gabe smiled. It was sort of frightening, even for him. "I'm not going to like this, am I?"

"Oh, it's fine. If he doesn't help, then I'll tell his mommy. She's scary." Vance pointed out that he thought she was as well. "Well, wait until you meet Edna. She'll make me look like the girl next door."

When she walked away, to call someone he thought, Vance looked at Dalton. He was staring at the door where Gabe had exited like a starved man. Vance said his name twice before he turned to him.

"Your mate, I think she might be a good fit with my company." Dalton nodded and smiled. "Christ, I hope I never ever meet my mate if you have to look all sappy like you do right now."

"I cannot wait until you meet her, Vance. You know what I'm going to do? I'm going to start taking notes on all the shit you tell me about not having a mate, and read them to her when she gets here." Vance growled. "Oh, you don't scare me anymore, buddy. I'll sic my wife-to-be on you and you'll go running with your tail between your legs."

Vance thought he might be right. Gabe didn't seem to be a pushover, nor did she appear to be afraid of him. Vance thought he might just like this sister best of all.

~~~

Gabe closed the phone and sat there quietly. She had a feeling that Vance wasn't going to be any happier with her now than he'd been before. The news she'd gotten wasn't good. In fact, it was downright scary. Turning when someone came in the room with her, Gabe smiled at the woman. Mrs. McCade had been in the kitchen since she'd shown up an hour ago.

"You get unpacked?" Nodding, she told her that she just had a few more things to sort out. "Oh good. How long will Vance be laid up?"

Gabe said nothing. She hadn't been aware that the woman knew her son was here, much less that he was hurt. But when she just cocked a brow at her Gabe closed her mouth tightly.

"My boys, all of them, think that I'm just this woman who raised them. I haven't any idea why they feel I can't handle a little bad news with the good. I've had a lot of the latter lately, just so you know. But they're my boys, and I know when they're hurt faster than they do at times. Not really, but I know." Gabe nodded. "Vance is the toughest boy I had, always has been. But as I said, he's my boy. And a mother knows things. Besides, I have resources that you cannot believe, so don't ever think to pull the wool over my eyes."

"I wouldn't dream of it." She thanked her and asked again about Vance. "I can't tell you anything. I made a promise. You have to understand that about me too since I decided to work for Kenton. I hold promises and secrets to my heart. I was asked to not say a word. To anyone. And I won't. Not even to you."

Aisha, what she'd been asked to call her, just sat there. She wasn't happy with what she'd said to her, Gabe could see that. But if she wanted to know something, anything about

Vance and his wounds, then she was going to have to ask the man himself.

"Is he all right now, at least?" Gabe nodded. "Do I need to know the rest? I know you won't tell me, and while I'm upset about that, I applaud you for keeping your promise."

"No, there is no reason for you to know anything other than he's fine." Aisha nodded. "Thank you."

"For what?" Gabe told her. "Honey, the fact that you're willing to help him, and not go running into the night, thrills me to no end. Also that you can be trusted with whatever anyone tells you. I love you for that as well."

"Well, I thank you for not asking me for too much." Aisha smiled. "I guess I need to get back to the bed and breakfast now. I mean, you know that I'm not really staying here, so I should get back."

"I thought you were staying here." Gabe told her she didn't even know whose home this was. "Dalton's. He bought it a few months ago. Well, this is his second home. I know that he also has one in town that he is renting right now. You should talk to him before you take off."

She had to talk to Vance too, but didn't tell her that. When Aisha started talking about dinner and what she should have made, Gabe wondered about the man upstairs. And what he'd want of her now.

Dalton wasn't like other men she'd dated. He was kind and strong. Most of the men she had gone out with over the last five years or so were doctors, men with huge egos and bigger demands on the women they dated. Like someone should simply have sex with them because they were who they were. And Dalton's family was nice.

"Gabe?" She looked at Vance, then around the room for his mom. "She's gone to the kitchen. Mom said that you sort of zoned out on her. She also said that you hadn't told her

37

anything."

"You told me not to. Is it safe to talk to you here? I can go outside if you'd like and tell you." He sat down slowly and told her now would be fine. "All right. I spoke to Jeff and I gave him the numbers that I found on the cylinder. He said that he'd get back with me by this evening."

"He can be trusted...you're sure about that?" Gabe nodded. "I don't trust many people, just my family, but if you say he can be trusted, then I will. But he knows to be careful with his computer if that's what he's using, yes?"

"Yes, he would know better than most. Jeff is...how shall I say this...? He's a hacker. And a very good one. You'd have read about him, I'm sure. He goes by the handle Prick Stick." Vance laughed. "Yes, well, he might be really smart, but he has no imagination. Anyway, he has this set up that will route him around the world a few times dinging his signal off a thousand sites and enabling him to be long gone before you ever find him. Plus, people underestimate him."

"Why?" She just shrugged. "Oh come on now, you've told me this much about him. What is it that makes people overlook him?"

"He's blind and confined to a wheelchair." She knew that Vance hadn't been expecting that, and continued before he could let it work around in his head. "About the time he and I became friends, he was living with his father. Jeff would spend half his time with his dad and the other time with his mom. His parents had never married. Jeffery, his dad, was a bastard. He would hurt Jeff whenever he had to pay for something that was required of him by law. You know, food, insurance, and clothing."

"Sounds like a winner. I bet his father wasn't thrilled when it turned out his son was gay either, was he?" Gabe said he was dead. "Good, saves me the trouble."

Gabe said nothing. She had wanted to kill the prick herself, but at the time she'd been a kid, not much older than Jeff. But she had decided to become a doctor after he was hurt. She looked at the china cabinet rather than Vance as she continued.

"Jeffery had a good job, and to the world he was a good provider as well as father. But he wasn't. And when his son never showed any interest in manly things—football, basketball, or any other sport—he would make him try out or play. It wasn't that he didn't care for sports, he just didn't want to play them." Gabe remembered the bruises and hurts on her friend, and had never once believed they were from playing as Jeff had wanted her to believe. "When Jeff was twelve, he invited me over to have dinner. It was just pizza and junk food, but we were having a blast. Then his father came home and the nanny who had been caring for us left."

She remembered what had happened next like a loop in her mind. Whenever she was exhausted or thinking about Jeff, she'd see it play out. She told Vance like she'd seen it, like she was still the little girl that had been caught up in a nightmare.

"Jeffery came home, like I said, and the nanny left. I'm not sure what that was about, but once she was gone, Jeff became quiet. It was strange to me, even then, to see him just become this other person. He could and still will talk your arm off if you don't shut him down. His dad came into the kitchen where we'd been eating and swiped all the food to the floor. Neither of us moved. 'Your coach called me at the office. He said that you didn't want to play soccer anymore. Why?' There wasn't time for Jeff to answer, his father had answered for him. 'Do you think it's too much for you? Does it hurt you to fall down?'"

His voice had taken on a whiny tone. His face was

39

contorted into this monstrous look that had her backing into her chair to get away from him. And when he asked Jeff again why he'd quit, Jeff looked at her.

"You have to go. Now. I don't want you hurt." It had been in that moment she'd known. Jeff was being hurt by his dad. "Go home, Gabe, please? I'll call you in a couple days and we'll go to the movies."

She hadn't left, of course, but had stood up on her chair and told Jeffery to go away. And when he laughed at her, she felt her temper snap. But she never got the chance to lash out at the man, even if she could have, because he'd slapped her. Hard enough to not just knock her off the chair, but to fly across the room and hit her head on the stove.

Gabe looked at Vance. "I woke up in the hospital. My dad was there, as was my sister. They were both crying, and I had no idea what had happened." Vance asked her what did happen. "Jeffery hit him, I guess harder than he had me. And when Jeff, a small kid anyway, hit the wall behind him, he crushed a part of his skull. But his father didn't stop there. When Jeff left the hospital, he was permanently blind and in a wheelchair because of a broken back."

"What did he find out?" She nodded and reached for the paper she'd made notes on. Vance put his hand over hers. "Thank you for telling me. And the next time you speak to him, ask him if he'd be willing to help me out on a few other things too. I'd pay him."

"I'll let him know." Clearing her throat, she picked up the paper. "It's a tracker, just like I thought it was. Jeff said that it's government issue, just as I'm also assuming you knew. The remote to it is in DC…he can't figure out who has it yet, but he will. And if the numbers are correct, and I read them to him four times, you don't want to have it removed. But he did suggest that you find out how many others you have in your body. He said he'd bet at least half a dozen."

"Did he say why that many?" She nodded. "I'm not going to like this answer, am I? Tell me so I can figure this out."

"He said that he thought there would be at least one in each arm, more than likely both legs too. You'd have one in your head somewhere, or the neck, as well as under a rib. That way if you were hurt badly enough to have something amputated, they'd still know where you were. Gruesome fuckers, don't you think?" She'd been going for a joke, but it fell flat. "He also said not to remove them. He's sure that there is something on them that can detect when they're fucked with. He's thinking that they're on a remote detonator, and that as soon as you mess with them or the people who had them inserted, they'll set them off and no more you. Jeff said that if you ever manage to get one taken out, for any reason, that he wants it. He likes to play with things like that. Oh, and they're only trackers, they can't hear whatever it is you say."

When he got up and left her, Gabe just sat there. She'd hate to be the person that put those things in Vance. He was a dead man, no doubt about that, and she had a feeling that it wouldn't be a quick one.

Shivering, she went to find Dalton. Gabe needed a nice guy to talk to her for a moment or two. Not that Vance wasn't nice, she supposed, but he wasn't like Dalton. Smiling as she made her way through the house, Gabe thought that no one was like Vance. And that was what made him so good at what he did. And Gabe knew what he did too, or had a good idea. Jeff had told her.

"He's elite, as in Special Forces elite. He's the guy they call in to do the bad things. Like murder for hire." Gabe had asked him how he'd come to that conclusion. "The government wants to know his every move. They don't put those kinds of things on agents or lawyers. This is to find a man that they're afraid of. They want to know when he's coming."

"You think that whoever had those put in him, they'll hurt him if they get the chance?" Jeff told her that they'd never catch him unless he wanted them to. "Why would he let them catch him?"

"To kill them."

Chapter 4

Caelin waited for Dalton to be calm. There was something amiss, something that Caelin couldn't help him with, so he waited. He did not want to disturb whatever thought process was going on with Dalton.

I can feel you there. Like a bad meal. What is it? Caelin told him that he could wait. *No, tell me. If you distract me enough, maybe I can figure out this scene. I have two people dead, and I'm not sure what happened other than what it's supposed to look like.*

I know not what that means, my lord, but I would like to ask you about the jewelry. Her ladyship hasn't put it to her flesh yet. I know what she has, but cannot clearly see what she is thinking. Dalton told him he thought that was the point of her not wearing them. *She thinks I will pest her.*

Pester, and yes, that's pretty much it. She said you bother her enough as it is. Gabriela said that if she were to put them in her hair that you'd never leave her alone. Is she right? Caelin didn't answer him, but he still laughed. *If it will help you I can have her open the box, though I have to tell you, I don't think I'm going to have any luck at all making her do anything she doesn't want to. It wasn't fair of you to send the gift to her office, don't you think?*

I did not send her anything. I don't know how she received it. Without the jewelry connected to her, I only know that she is close to it and nothing more. Who did she say sent it to her? He told

43

him what he knew. *I don't know a Mr. Peterson. Nor the name Waterson. I will have to search to see what I can find out.*

You do that. In the meantime, what can you tell me about the men chasing her? There are a couple of different groups, I think. He told him that he only knew that she'd been shot at, nothing more. *There was a boy too, I don't know if she ever told me his name, but he was related to Waterson. Grandson, I think.*

Caelin really was limited to what he knew because she refused to wear the hair combs. She was most stubborn. There were only three pieces left; the brooch—which Caelin had a feeling was going to be the hardest to find—the necklace, and the hair combs that the lady Gabe had. He wondered briefly if he'd been mistaken about her having the combs, and dismissed that almost immediately. He could speak to her now, and the only way that could work was if she was the mate to one of the dragons.

I will search. If you could perhaps get the young miss to open the box and maybe touch it for me, I can tell you what its powers are. Sometimes there are others than just what I have a knowledge of. As you know, the more of the pieces that are brought to your family, the stronger you get. And those that wish to have them, they are getting desperate as well. Dalton said he had figured that out too. *Also, my lord, the reason that I have connected with you today, is I have been contacted by two dragons.*

I'm sorry, what? He repeated himself. *What do you mean, you've been contacted by other dragons? I didn't know there were others. Are they related to us?*

In a way. They're dragons, sir. As I am. He knew the moment that Dalton realized what he was saying. *I'm sorry, sir, I thought you knew there would be others coming.*

Here? They're coming here? Caelin felt Dalton's stress level rise, and wasn't sure how to handle it. *What are we going to do with dragons coming to visit?*

44

I think they mean to live there, sir. Dalton told him he wasn't helping. *I'm sorry. But you must give them permission to come here. They cannot come without it. I tried to ask Lord Kenton, but he is busy with a surgery. And Lord Jorden is working as well, and has threatened me should I bother him when he is painting. He said that I mess with his muse and he'll murder me when I come forth for doing so.*

And Grady? What's he doing that he can't be bothered? Caelin wasn't going to tell him the man was having sex. Again. He and his missus seemed to be constantly having sex. *Caelin?*

He is procreating. It was nicer to say that, Caelin thought, then the other term that he'd heard the men say. *Should I bother him now, I think he will do me harm. Lord Jorden has given me enough to worry with, but I think young Grady will...he was most explicit in what he would do to me.*

Laughter burst from Dalton's mouth. He could feel it, the good humor that washed over the man. It made Caelin smile, gave him a nice feeling all over his body. And when he still laughed a few minutes later, Caelin hated to beg again for an answer.

Tell them to come here. I'm not sure what we'll do with them, but tell them they'll be welcome. As much as we can make them, anyway. But not to come all at once. We can hide them better one at a time rather than two. All right? Caelin said that he would tell them. *Now, I have to solve this case or I'm not going to get to go home and try to procreate myself. If I can talk my mate into it.*

Touch something that you cannot see. Dalton asked him what that meant. *Is there a weapon? Blood perhaps? If you touch something that you cannot...not see, but I mean, you cannot believe it to be right. Touch it and you can see it.*

The moment that he touched the item, Caelin felt it as well. He could see what the dead man had, seen the killer's face, as well as everything that had happened just before he'd been killed. Caelin knew, too, that Dalton was aware of who the murderer was, and the reason that he'd done such a horrific thing.

Can my brothers do this too, touch something and see what happened to it? Caelin told him he thought so, but hadn't been sure it would work until then. *Is it the jewelry you think, what Gabriela brought here?*

I would say yes. If this is the magic that came with them, it would be the hair combs. They will strengthen the blood that flows through you, thus enhancing your powers of perception. Dalton asked him how. *Your blood is stronger, richer from the magic. And in turn, it will flow faster over your mind, heart, and brain. That will bring stronger awareness to you. The ability to touch and feel, another trait with richer blood, is that you're more sensitive to those things you touch.*

Everything? Caelin told him that things like spilled blood or violence with a weapon would have the most power. The rest, he'd feel something, but it might not always be so clear. *I'll get her to open the box tonight. This is.... I'm not sure if I should be freaked out or happy about this. It will certainly make my job a great deal easier, for as long as I work at it anyway.*

Caelin thanked him and left him to his job. He had stuff to do as well; Caelin was also preparing things. If the hair combs were indeed in the box, then that left only the brooch and necklace to be brought here. He knew that Grady and Harper could find them and bring them to the safety of the McCades, but to do so would mess with the events that would come from the women finding them. There had to be mates with them to make the magic work. Caelin curled into his form and thought.

The McCades had suffered so much over the years. More than he thought that even the queen had envisioned. He saw her now, in his thoughts. The stronger the men got with the jewelry, the more he was remembering. Warrior, he'd been called so long ago, and the child that he'd been set to protect was the real Caelin.

The queen's child had been a wonder to him. A smaller version of his mother, strong and full of magic, he'd been kind to Warrior. Never pulling at his scales. Not teasing him with his tail. Warrior even remembered the days leading up to his departure from the castle. The queen had trained young Caelin, then had taken Warrior's magic, all of him, and separated it into the jewels to save for the boy. Warrior had given his life for the child, and would do so again if necessary.

"You will need to be a great warrior, my son. Someone that will carry the seeds of your family for generations to come." He'd been but a child, no more than seven or so, when he nodded at his mother. "I know that it is a great deal to ask of you…you should be playing with other kids, enjoying your childhood. But should he find you, he will kill you."

"I will avenge your exile, my mother." It had surprised them both that he knew. That a child hidden away from his father from his first breath would have known that his sire was a monster. And that he was going to try and murder his mother. "You will be safely hidden away and I will come for you. Someday, we will be together."

Women of this world were nothing like the ones of his time. Not that he was disappointed in them. Nay, they were stronger for their years. And sassier as well. Smiling, he thought of the young miss that had joined them, and her telling him off. He knew that phrase now; Dalton had explained it to him.

She is stubborn to a fault. Dalton had told him that she was indeed that. *I think you believe this to be funny. I was simply telling her how much more I could do for her if she would just wear the jewelry, and she was very cross with me.*

47

She told you off. He asked him the meaning. *Well, you wanted her to do something that went against anything that she believes in. Or that she felt comfortable with. So she told you – not so nicely, I'm betting – to leave her alone, that she had a handle on it, and that she made her own decisions.*

Do not forget that she said that I was a pain in her ass. I was nowhere near that part of her person, nor would I ever be. What a thing to say to someone who is only trying to help her. Dalton wanted to know if he'd asked her or had he bullied her.

He'd learned the difference then…not only that he'd been bullying all the women, but that he'd been very annoying, a word that he'd never been called before in his lifetimes. But he could see that he hadn't been the best of help to any of them. Caelin had information for them, even ideas at times, but Dalton had explained to him that it was his execution of how he gave out the things he knew that was the problem.

What I'd do, and this would be just me, I'd tell one of us whatever it is you've found out and ask them to tell the others. You know as well as I that you've interrupted some private times with my brothers. And have talked over them when they're having a conversation with someone who might not know about you. Unless it's extremely important, I think it's safe to say it can wait. Caelin asked for an example. *Yesterday when I was working on that case, you knew I was busy. Yet you wanted to let me know that you'd found a flower that you'd long since thought to be dead.*

I see. My excitement does not mean you will feel the same. Dalton told him that he thought it was wonderful about the flower; however, Caelin's timing was off. *Yes, I can see that now. I will contain myself better.*

And he had, too. It wasn't even as hard as he thought it might be. And everyone seemed genuinely happy to hear his information when he had it because he had not stressed them out. That was what he'd been doing, he knew this.

Oh my lady. Where are you when I need you? He knew, however, or at least he thought he did. She had merged her magic to that of Lady Harper. And when her female child was born and her name bestowed upon her, the child would be the greatest witch of all time. A new Prisane would be born.

~~~

Gabe watched Harper work. It was amazing to her to see a ball of clay formed into a tall cylinder. And even more fascinating was the fact that when she was finished getting it to the height that she wanted, Harper would, using only a sponge, make the shape something new and wonderful. When Shawn fussed a little, she realized she was paying less attention to his needs than she should have been.

"I appreciate you feeding him while I work. I wanted to get these four pieces thrown today and let them dry out. Jorden was here earlier, but he got called away." Gabe told her that she was enjoying herself. "I'm sure you are. Isn't it amazing that a little baby can make a person, an otherwise normal adult, turn into such a sap?"

"Yes, even Aisha. She is this strong, vibrant woman who can tear into someone like she's hell on wheels. I mean, I've witnessed it, so I know what I'm talking about. That salesman that came to her door will think twice before he knocks on a door again, I think. But once she has Shawn in her arms, she's this mushy, insane woman who can't even talk above a whisper. Not to mention, the goofy expressions on her face."

"You mean like you have now?" Gabe laughed and kissed the baby on its fat cheek. "Have you noticed how many pregnant women there are around? I mean, sheesh, it's like it's in the water around here or something. And they're so different in the way they handle everything. I was just cumbersome and clumsy. Some of these ladies, I bet they could walk a tight wire and never fall."

49

They both agreed the pack women appeared to have it right. They never seemed to have swollen ankles, they were fit and strong, and one of them, when she'd examined her a couple of days ago, had told Gabe that when she had her baby, she was headed right back to work. Gabe thought it was a shifter thing.

"There were three women on my staff that got pregnant at the same time. One of them was an old pro at it—she had three others at home—but the other two were as different as night and day during it." She thought of the women and smiled. "Carly was younger, and I'm sure that had a lot to do with it, but she would run circles around the rest of us, sit down and literally pass out for a few minutes, then get up and do it all again. Sharon, she was a pampered girl…her parents had done everything for her when she'd been younger, and she would whine and complain about every little change in her body. Oh, and she would measure her belly several times a day. I think she was overly worried about getting her body back."

The noise downstairs made them both grow still.

"You expecting anyone?" Harper said she wasn't, that she'd locked the door when they came in. "Okay, that reaching thing…tell someone what's going on, and take Shawn to the other room."

"What about you?" Gabe said that she was used to this more than she might be. "Used to what? Break-ins?"

"Yes."

Helping Harper into the office, telling her to hide under the desk, Gabe pulled her gun from her purse. She had no idea if she could actually use it on anyone, but she sure as shit wasn't going to wish she had it when the shit hit the fan. Going to the stairwell, Gabe made sure that she was well back in the event they looked up.

The man was dressed all in black. Gabe started to shout down to him that she had a gun when she saw the other two. She might have been able to scare one person, but three? Not so much. Gabe nearly screamed when Caelin spoke to her.

I should like to help you. She told him she'd take all she could get right now. *Thank you, my lady. You have the ability to call the dragons.*

I.... You know what? I don't care how I have that, but you go ahead and tell me how to get them. He paused. *Caelin, Shawn is here, and so is Harper. I'd very much like to be the hero and not the dead one either.*

You don't have the gift on your person. Those fucking hair things? He was bringing that up again? Before she could tell him to fuck off, he spoke once more. *They give you the strength that you need, my lady. The ability to call the dragons. Also to heal faster. You will need them, now more than ever before, if this should turn out badly.*

If you're lying to me I'm going to be really pissed off. He told her that he could no more lie to her than he could any of the others. *All right. I'm doing this, but I swear to you, Caelin, I'm not happy.*

She made her way to her purse, careful of not making any noises that would alert them that she was doing anything. Pulling out the box that Peterson had given her, Gabe tried to think how best to put them in. Taking them out of the box, her breath caught when she saw them for the first time.

They were wings. The wings of a dragon, she'd bet her last nickel. And as she pulled them out of the box, one at a time, she felt the first jolt of power. It frightened and excited her at the same time. Clipping the first one into her hair, she knew the moment that the others felt it; their connection to her was tight, unbreakable. And when the second one was sitting upon her head, Gabe had to hold onto the table so as

51

not to fall over as the strength of something washed over her.

She looked in the mirror near the stairs and could only stare at her reflection. The hair combs were now blue streaks in her hair. From the top to the very bottom, a dark two-inch-wide strip of blue glistened in the overhead lighting. And Gabe would bet anything it would be there for the rest of her…for what she hoped was a very long life.

Going to the stairs again, she looked down. Gabe couldn't see anyone, but when she closed her eyes, not only did she see the men there, but she knew what they'd come there for as well; to kill the baby and take both her and Harper. Uttering the words that she knew instinctively would bring her the dragons, Gabe held her breath and waited.

They were just suddenly there. She touched them both, ran her fingers along their heads and felt the connection. It was so strong that she wondered for a moment if she'd turned into one of them. But almost as soon as the thought entered her head, she knew it was because of the magic of the jewels.

"There are three or more men downstairs that are going to kill the baby and then hurt Harper and I. Do you know what to do?" The larger of the two dragons nodded. "Just…I was going to tell you to be careful, but I think you'll be just fine."

We will save you all. She nodded and moved back when the dragons flew down the stairs. Gabe was wondering if she should follow them or not when Harper quietly called her name.

"He left me." Gabe asked her what she meant. "My dragon. Grady and I, we each have a dragon that moves over our bodies, and it…. What did you do?"

"I don't…are you hurt? Did…? I have no idea. Caelin told me that I could call the dragons to me. I thought…I guess I assumed that he meant the McCades. Then these little guys showed up and—"

The scream from below them was cut off. There was a crash, the sound of gunfire. Then silence. Harper grabbed her hand, and they were headed back to the other room when the dragons were in the room with them, this time sitting on the floor.

They were no bigger than a medium sized dog. Their wings, she knew, made them appear much larger, but they were far from as cuddly as a dog would be. Each of them had sharp spikes at their backs, and horns on their heads. The larger of the two was bluer than the other...not darker, just bluer. There were other differences between the two, but all she wanted to know now was how they had helped.

"What happened to the men?" Neither of them said anything, but she knew, as surely as she was standing there, they were all dead. "What will the police say when they show up? I mean, if you killed them. I need to come up with a story that won't have them taking me away in a straitjacket, nor have me put to death by lethal injection."

They are no more. Gabe looked at Harper, then back at the dragons. *You will be safe. No one will ever know that they were here, my lady. I know of this straitjacket you speak of, but you should rest assured that you'll never be put in one of them. Nor will anyone kill you for the death of those men.*

She wasn't sure what to say at this point. The men were dead, and she was uncharacteristically happy. It was her job to make sure that people lived, not to be thrilled when they were killed. Of course, these men had been more than willing to kill her and Harper, and the baby, but right now, she didn't want to think of that. Instead, she thought of how they'd come to her.

"You belong to Harper and Grady, don't you? I mean, you're the dragons that were on their bodies? Harper said that you were gone from her. You didn't harm her when you left her, did you? I mean, she'll be all right without you there?"

The dragons looked at one another, then nodded. *Yes, my lady, they are both unharmed because we have left them. But we belong to no one. We serve you all.* She asked him if only she could call them. *I know not, my lady. We are here to serve you and the others, in any way that we can.*

"So what happens to you now?" He asked Harper what she meant. Gabe wondered as well. "You've come to our aid. Killed those men before they hurt us or killed my son. Do you get into trouble because of that? I mean, do you have someone to answer to?"

Also, did she send them back? Did they have to find a place for them to live? How would they account for missing men, if it ever came up? There were so many questions running through her head, and for every one that she thought of, Gabe was sure that there were ten times that many that would eventually come up.

The only one we answer to is the McCade family. No one rules us but you. We have helped. Now that you are safe, we will return. Before she could ask him where that might be to, they disappeared. Looking at Harper, Gabe knew that hers was back on her body.

"That is some fucked up shit." Harper laughed. "I don't know about you, but I could use a drink. I don't even care that it's only ten in the morning."

"If I wasn't still nursing Shawn, I might join you. But I do think we need to go and see what happened downstairs. Oh, and the men are on their way. For whatever reason, I wasn't able to contact them. But Grady said he was on his way with Dalton and the others. I don't think he's really thrilled about any of this either. Mostly he's pissed that he didn't know you were in danger and couldn't help you."

Great, she thought. She'd just ordered the hit of several men, and she wasn't even sure what had happened to them. Dalton was pissed off because.... Well, she wasn't really positive why he was upset that she'd taken care of the problem on her own, but there it was. And she'd summoned two dragons to her. Gabe wondered if anything else could go wrong today.

CHAPTER 5

Dalton wasn't sure if he should be impressed or terrified. Right now he was sandwiched between both emotions. He was really glad that Gabe had been there to help Harper and the baby, scared shitless that there were not just men that had made it that close to his family, and that Gabriela had been able to call dragons to help them.

"You okay?" Dalton just glared at Jorden. "Well, you do look a little off. I mean, they're all okay."

"Yes, they're all okay. Because my mate could call dragons to her. Dragons that more than likely killed those three men and then got rid of the bodies. Do you have any idea what someone would do if they saw that security surveillance video? I can tell you, they'd freak the fuck out right before they took us all away and threw away the key. Not to mention, there is no blood. Not a single drop of it, nor a trace of the men." Jorden just cocked his brow at him, and Dalton realized how loud he'd gotten. "I'm sorry. I'm just...I haven't any idea what to think right now. I'm just, all right."

"Yes, but you have to talk to Gabe. I would suggest you do it when you're calmer. She's upset enough." Dalton glanced at Gabe and asked Jorden what had happened. "You. Mostly you, anyway. She just killed those men. And no matter how you try and pretty it up for her that they were going to kill

57

them, she still had a heavy hand in making it happen. And instead of going to her and telling her how brave she was, smart enough to save not just herself but Harper and the baby too, you're over here acting like a fucking baby because those men are dead. Men that I'd like to point out to you again were set on killing Shawn and taking the women. Your mate, one of them."

"I'm sorry." Jorden told him he was saying that to the wrong person. "I don't know what to do, Jorden. I want to protect her, but there is only just so much I can do without knowing what we're up against all the time. And it's not like we have any clue about it either. Men that hate dragons have been trying to kill our mates for generations. I think it would really suck to have gone through all this and then it ends just like the other lives have."

"What do you mean? You mean we die and this starts all over?" Dalton said that was what he'd been thinking. "Christ. But you're just a bag of jolly thoughts, aren't you? Why would you even say something like that? Are you fucking serious right now? What is wrong with you?"

"I'm fucking in love with her." He looked around, because he knew he'd been a little loud. "I'm in love with her, and I don't think she even likes me."

"I wouldn't." Jorden laughed when he told him to fuck off. "Dalton, what is it you want? From her? Because as far as I can see, you're not making any kind of effort to do anything about even the simplest of things. Like, where is she living?"

"At my house." Dalton flushed. "Okay, she's staying there, I guess you could call it. I don't have a lot of interaction with her either. I know that, but I've been sort of busy since Howard passed away."

"Too busy that you'd neglect your mate to do a job you told me last week you were going to quit? And she's not living with you or staying there. As far as I know, she's still at the B&B. Also, and this is the funny one, she has no idea what to do about you either. I'd kick your ass, but that's just me." Dalton wanted to tell him to mind his own business, but he was right. "Dalton, did you know that she told Kenton that she didn't think her working with him was going to work out? That she might be looking to move on?"

"No. Really?"

Jorden nodded, then walked away. Dalton stood there, his heart hurting. As he made his way to her, he could see the tear stains on her face. The sadness in her eyes. He simply pulled her into his arms and held her. Dalton felt her shoulders shake as she wrapped her arms around his neck. Christ, she really was upset. Holding her, he watched as the rest of his family left them. Dalton lifted up Gabe's chin to look at her when they were alone. "I'm so sorry."

"I had them killed...those men are dead because of me. I don't kill, Dalton, I'm a doctor. I heal people, not have them murdered." He kissed her, just a gentle touching of their lips. And when he lifted his head, she smiled at him. "That was really nice. A great way to distract me from what I've done. Will you visit me in prison and do that?"

"No one is going to prison." When she started to no doubt protest, he kissed her again. This time he put a little more need in it. Dalton brushed her hair from her face and ran his fingers over the silky blue tresses that she now had. "I've not been a very attentive mate. And this is really pretty. The combs, I'm guessing."

"Yes. In order to call the dragons to me, I have to be wearing them. Attentive? I don't even know what that means. But I sure could use a little pep talk if you have it in you." He kissed her again, this time pulling her body closer to his. Then when she wrapped her arms around his neck tighter, Dalton

59

cupped her ass and brought her flush to his cock. "Dalton, I've been lonely for a long time. So unless you plan on doing something about my neediness, then you should really walk away."

"What would you like for me to do to help you with this problem you seem to have?" She giggled and he rocked into her again. "A man offers his services up and you laugh? Gabriela, you have wounded me."

"Please, just call me Gabe. I had a boss call me Gabriela, and I didn't like him overly much. But every time you touch me, get close enough to touch me, I feel as if you've set me…I don't want to talk about fire." He nodded and kissed her again, this time lifting her up so that she could wrap around him. "Dalton, please. You have no idea what this is doing to me."

"I do. I really do. What if I wanted you to lie back, to let me strip you down so that I could feast on you?" Her moan nearly had him tossing her to the table to do just as he'd threatened. "I'm going to enjoy this, I think."

After laying her over the table that was used to weigh up clay balls, he sat down so he could take his time touching her. Dalton lifted her leg up to his face and nipped at her ankle. Taking off her shoe, he massaged her foot with one hand and slid the other up her leg.

Her skin was warm and smooth, and when he touched the back of her knee, she moaned again. Kissing her ankle, licking his way up her leg, he felt his cock strangle in his pants and had to adjust himself before he did some major damage. But he couldn't seem to get enough of her. Not her scent, her taste, or the sounds that she made when aroused.

Laying her leg down, Dalton leaned over her, pulling her shirt up off her belly with his teeth. Her breath was harsh, warm as it blew over his face. And when he licked her belly button, then bit into her flesh, her fingers curled in his hair and jerked him up.

"Stop playing and get to work." He pulled her hand free. "Dalton, I'm seriously overheated right now. If you don't help me out, I'm going to do it myself."

"I'd love to watch that." He put his hands into the top of her pants and sat up, taking them off her as he did so. "However, I have some exploring to do here. And I'd really appreciate it if you didn't keep distracting me."

Pulling her pants off, Dalton dropped them to the floor. He'd left her panties on, but he could see how wet they were. He wanted to taste her there, see if she tasted as good as she smelled, but he wanted to see her, all of her, before he started making love to her.

Her blouse was next. Dalton wasn't as easy on it as he had been with her pants. There wasn't any way for him to remove it without her help, so he simply tore it open. Pressing his thumb hard against the wettest part of her panties, Dalton was hoping to bring her relief as well as a lot of pleasure. He thought he'd done a pretty good job of it, too, when she bowed up off the table and cried out.

"Did you enjoy that, love?" Her nodding, then the shaking of her head, had him smiling. "Yes, well, since you can't decide, perhaps I can help you with another short blow to your system."

He slid his hand up her thigh, watching her face as he did so. When she looked like she was going to cry out again, he slid his fingers under the elastic on her panties and into her heat.

The way she screamed was wonderfully fulfilling to him. She told him she was coming again a sort second later, so he leaned into her apex and bit her clit through her panties. This time when she came, she held him to her body and rode his mouth. Dalton needed more, and moved the scrap of material out of his way and suckled her clit into his mouth as she came three more times in quick punching order.

Her panties had to go, and making short work of them by tearing them off her as well seemed the quickest way. Lifting her leg up to his shoulder, Dalton licked her clit before taking her nether lips and all into his mouth and devouring her. He was rewarded with so much of her cream that he could barely keep up with the flow of it. And every time she came, his mouth filled.

Dalton ate her voraciously. He loved everything about her. The way she shivered after each release. The way her fingers would go limp for several seconds after she came. The sounds that she made when she was coming down. The heat of her skin, the way she begged him for more in one moment then pleaded with him to stop the next.

When he couldn't wait any longer, he stood up. Her body was heaving, her bra had been pushed up over her breasts, and her hands were cupping the beautiful orbs. He wanted those as well, to taste her pink nipples until she begged him to stop. To suckle at them, taking as much as he could into his mouth and biting down hard. Freeing his cock, Dalton stood over her and watched her. He fisted his cock, the achiness of it making his head spin.

"I want to feel you inside of me." He nodded and spread her legs wider and stepped between them. "I need you, Dalton. Please, fill me."

"Not yet." She sobbed at him to please fuck her. "I need to watch you come. I want to see how your breasts swell, your breathing stops. Show me, Gabe, show me how you come for me." Her left hand moved to her pussy, her right pulled hard at her nipples. Just when he thought he couldn't take anymore of her teasing, she slid her fingers inside and screamed.

Dalton wasn't prepared for how quick, how consuming her climax had been. Even as he fisted his cock, he knew he was finished. As soon as she cried out the second time in as many seconds, he came too, spraying his cum all over her body and face.

Christ, he thought, he was going to die. He felt it to his toes. The way his body released had him thinking that he'd have no more, nothing to give her until weeks from now. But as long as he was standing there, her body spread out before him, Dalton was going to take all of her. Pulling her to the edge of the table, he slammed his cock into her and leaned down to take her breast. Distracted for a moment, he fucked her slowly, watching her face once again.

"I love you, Gabe. With all my heart." He moved inside of her, taking her as close to coming as he could before backing off. "When I come in you, I want to feel you tighten around me. I need to see your face when you release."

"Please, Dalton. I need that and more." He asked her what else he could give her. "Everything. I want it all. Please, you're the only one that can give it to me."

And he wanted her to have it. Pounding her now, giving as much as he was taking from her, he licked a path from her breast to the throbbing pulse at her throat. As soon as she tightened around him, her sheath milking his cock, Dalton let go.

His body seemed to be poised for a few seconds when he released, like it was waiting. And when he came, he knew it had been for her, for the moment they came together on so many levels.

It was epic, literally like the epi center of something major. Dalton threw back his head, his body bowing with it as he climaxed. He had not a single thought as he emptied deep within her. He could feel her, the way she came with him, but there was nothing in this world that could have prepared him for the feelings that came with their union.

They were one. Mate to mate. Husband and wife. And Dalton knew that from this moment on, she would be his everything. And he would give himself to her from now on. Dalton was deeply and forever in love with Gabe McCade.

~~~

She wasn't the right woman. And worse than that, she didn't have the jewelry on her. Not even a fucking watch. Ronny kicked the woman in the head and screamed at her. The fucking bitch; it wasn't right that she was the wrong one again.

Ronny pulled out the picture that he'd found on the interwebbers. He knew that wasn't what it was called, but he said that to keep people from giving him much in the way of second looks. But he knew...Ronny Webbers was the smartest man alive.

He grinned. Okay, he wasn't, but he had high test scores to prove he was at least a little more intelligent than the average Joe. And he'd worked really hard at becoming the smartest ever been born. But if he was honest with himself, and he usually was, he was bored with that shit. That was how he'd come across the legend of the McCade's Millions.

It dated back for centuries. Probably even before there was printed information that he could locate. It dealt with dragons, of all things, kings and queens, as well as magic. Ronny decided that he'd very much like to see about this magic angle, and that was the only reason that he'd dug deeper into this thing and found out about the jewelry and what it was supposed to do when it was all together. He'd been so surprised by how much he'd been able to unearth on the subject that he'd devoted an entire room to it.

All the information that he could find, right at his

fingertips. And there was a great deal of it too. Where the last of the McCades lived, which surprisingly wasn't that far from him. How long they'd been looking and what happened on the failed attempts. He had charts, notes, as well as photographs of all the men he could find. And that was another thing about this that surprised him; there had only been sons born of the family in all their recorded history.

Ronny had at first thought about going to their home and showing them all that he'd been able to find. Sort of be their partner in it. He wanted a payoff, of course…some kickback for what he knew. But in the end, he'd decided that he'd rather just have it all than to have to share. That was the mistake the other people looking for this crap had made, and it had been their downfall. Like recently.

A man by the name of Fredrick Winslow had found a few of the pieces. He might even had been close to getting a couple more when he met with a very violent and untimely death. There had been speculation that he'd been a little off his rocker at the end. According to the paper, he'd been involved in a murder-suicide that had ended his family name as well. Ronny didn't believe that for a minute.

"Pop," he said to himself as he held his finger to his head. "You're all dead." And if they didn't play ball with him, the way he wanted, then they'd be just as dead as the several generations before them. He would end them all.

Ronny got into his car and made his way to his home as he thought of the most recent guy. Ollie Morrison had been a foolish idiot if he thought his way of getting the jewels was going to happen. Bargaining with the devil never worked out, he thought.

Of course Morrison was dead now. His body had rolled up on the evening news one night after Ronny had begun this thing, and he knew just what had happened. Really, what the paper had written, as well as the evening news, had been a lie. Ronny had a pretty good idea of the truth, and instead of making him nervous about things, it made him giddy with anticipation. He was going to win this thing.

Morrison had been killed, that much was true. He'd gotten too close and someone had killed him. Didn't matter to Ronny who or how they'd done it, so long as they stayed out of his way. He just needed to find out who Morrison's buyer had been, and make sure that he wasn't searching for them on his own. Ronny was going to be the one to collect on all that magic, or he'd simply kill those that didn't agree with him.

As soon as he entered his bedroom, he looked at his notes. There were things there, information that he was fairly certain no one had found yet. The more pieces that came together, the fairy tale said, the stronger it got. He supposed that was why Ollie had been killed. The magic was just too strong, and it had called to other forces to make sure that he didn't end it before it began. While he wasn't sure what that meant, the beginning of this, he knew that he had to be the one that all this came to a head for.

Ronny wasn't going to mess around with kidnappings. Nor was he going to go in and try to get the pieces that were already with the McCade men. They were fine where they were for the time being. And the best part was, he knew just who had what piece because of his research. And he had a little information about what each piece was supposed to do when it was with the McCades.

The oldest man had the heart. He was sure of this, because according to the research he'd been doing, the oldest would wake the dragon with the ring. The second man—the birth order mattered little after the heart had woken—would have had the torques. Strength was supposed to come to the bringer of those. Ronny hadn't read what that might entail, but he was willing to bet it would be a lot of strength.

Strength of mind? Of body? He didn't know. But what he did know was that there had been a specific order of things through the generations, and he had made a lot of notes on that.

The third piece would have been the necklace. Again, like the torques, the information was vague on what exactly was supposed to come from it. Just that it would be information vital to the well-being. The well-being of the family? Of the dragon that was supposed to be awakened from this? He just figured that they'd have this special knowledge that he knew would do them very little good. They weren't going to be around long enough to get to that part, and only he would know how to decipher it.

The brooch would be found next, and that was what he was looking for now. That sucker was supposed to be worth millions in both gems and jewels. It would also bring the man who owned it armor. Ronny had an idea that it wasn't an army to protect, but some kind of shield that they could use to protect against all manner of weapons.

Since it had been lifetimes since anyone had actually seen the pieces together, he wasn't completely sure what they looked like. There were drawings of them, a few pictures that he had a feeling were fakes, as well as descriptions from questionable sources that said they'd seen them. Perhaps, like most legends, the story was sort of a mishmash of the things that he'd been able to unearth. The hair combs, for example. The keeper of those was supposed to be able to call dragons to them. Dragons? Not likely.

"Like somewhere in this world there are dragons just lying about until this guy calls them." He laughed. "I'm pretty sure that at some time, somewhere, there would have been a sighting of fucking dragons."

Then there were the earrings. They had been the last piece to be found by the others. And as such, there was the least amount of information to be found about them. Since all the pieces had to be together to call forth the great riches of money and dragons, that last piece had never come to light. Or so he'd been able to surmise, as he couldn't find anything about them.

Ronny figured that he had to work the hardest to find where it was first, so that when it came to the end of this thing, he'd be able to say he them. The earrings were said to be the most beautiful things ever forged. Ronny smiled when he thought of the looks on the McCades' faces when he produced them.

The information about the brooch was wrong, so he had to start over with it. The woman that he'd had to kill knew no more about it than he did. And that had pissed him off royally.

Tearing down the map and notes he had on the woman, he looked at the writings in his notebook. He had a feeling... and Ronny had no idea why, that someone was out there thwarting his efforts. And that just would not do.

He knew that Morrison had a buyer. But who he was, where he lived, wasn't anything he could find. The computer hacker that he knew wasn't all that helpful, and he might have killed him if he knew more about the little cocksucker. His handle should have been helpful, but all that gave him was more heartache.

By the time dinner was being called, Ronny was no closer to finding the brooch than he'd been before. There was conflicting information on it, first of all. And again, he had a feeling that someone was misguiding him. He nearly closed the book on his information when he saw a small sheet of paper sticking out of the edge of one of the many books he'd gotten from an estate sale not long ago.

"'Riddle, riddle on the wall, what do you know that I cannot tell?'" Ronny sat down. The paper was old. Or it was meant to look that way. The handwriting was also very fancy, script like he'd seen in another book that he'd found. He read the rest of the words on the paper out loud. "'Dragon dragon, blue and white, how will you hide so well from me?' Stupid. It's either a childish poem or something else that is supposed to keep me off the prize."

He nearly tossed it in the trash, but instead turned it to its other side. There was a date and a name.

The year was sixteen hundred and ten. Ronny wasn't sure it was right or not, but he got out his magnifying glass to see if the name — he was sure that was what it was — was more easily readable. It wasn't a name that he could pronounce. Even putting it in his translator, all he got was mumbling. Ronny was sure that he'd missed a letter or two, and spent the rest of the evening on that.

He worked for several hours, only stopping long enough to have a little dinner. But he had letters now, and was thrilled with the chase of it. Most of them he'd had to guess at. The fine script writing had them running all together, so he had no idea if the letter was an *e* or a *g*. He leaned back in his seat and closed his eyes. Maybe he just needed a break.

The year intrigued him. One of the notes that he'd been able to find on the interwebbers had mentioned the same year. He couldn't remember what they'd said right now, but he had extensive notes and would find it. But the name…he was sure that there had been no mention of a name. Getting up, only just realizing that he was starved, he decided that he'd call the university in the morning and ask them to first verify that it was indeed old paper, and then have them help him with the writing. He'd donated enough of his money there when he'd been a student, he thought they owed him.

Ronny didn't really donate. He didn't have the money for donations…barely enough for food most of the time. Moving back home into his mother's house had been hard on him. Harder still was that she had taken on boarders and he had to share his space with ten other people. And no matter how often he begged her, pleaded with her to kick them out, all she'd told him was if he paid her what he owed her, then she could give him the house and she'd spend her retirement years being waited on, not waiting on others.

Of course he wasn't ever going to pay her back. Christ, she had lent him that money over ten years ago to finance his first venture in becoming something. She had to move on. He had when it failed. And he blamed that on her as well. Had she been able to help him more, like lending him more money, he was sure that his business would have made it.

It had been a long shot he was willing to take. Selling the air above fields for businesses to transmit their information over had been brilliant. Why the bank had not seen it his way was beyond him. They were missing out on a lot of revenue. He was sure that they were secretly envious of his idea, and after he'd left the bank had gone on to start selling it on their own. Fucking bastards.

It was the reason he'd gone to his mom. It wasn't like she was going to live long enough to spend all the cash he knew she had. And he only wanted sixty-five percent of it. Still, what she had given him, not loaned, was not even a drop in the bucket he could have had if she'd just sold everything she had, including the house, and helped her only child out.

As he made his way to the kitchen to get him something for dinner, he thought of what he had to do to get the university to help him. Of course, he'd caused a bit of a stink when he'd been asked to leave when he was a student, so maybe he'd need to have really good reasons for asking them for help. Also, there was that little problem with their computers that he'd been guilty of. Ronny couldn't remember all the details about what he had done to completely erase not only their roster, but also all the grades of every student that had ever gone there. Ronny had said he was sorry, but they were still holding a grudge.

When he turned on the light to the kitchen, he stopped.

"Mother fuck. Now what did you go and do a thing like that for?"

His mother had put a lock on not just the refrigerator door, but also the pantry and cabinets he knew housed all the food he liked. Ronny figured that she would blame it on the other tenants when he began his midnight raids. His hope was that she'd kick them all out and be done with this thing. But she'd thought of other ways to keep them out, and this wasn't going to work for him. Ronny and his mom were going to have a little talk about this. In the morning. Christ, would she ever just die?

CHAPTER 6

Dalton looked over the paperwork in front of him. He knew what it was, but he was having a hard time thinking why anyone would think that he'd just blindly sign off on them. He looked at the attorney from the state offices, and asked him again why they wanted him to become the sheriff.

"Well, for one thing, you were recommended by Howard. Secondly, and this is the most important, you're damned good at your job. We know that you and Howard had an understanding. You'd do the job for him when he was away or needed some time off. It was a smooth transition between the two of you. We liked that."

Dalton leaned back in the chair he'd been sitting in for the last couple of hours, and wondered where Gabe was. He'd been doing that a lot the last few hours, just wondering what she was doing and how she was liking working with Kenton. His brother had told him not to bother him every ten seconds just a little while ago. He supposed he was being a pain in the ass, but he missed her and didn't want to make her think he was too clingy. It was the reason that he'd bothered his brother and not her. Now this idiot wanted him to take over a job that not two weeks ago he'd wanted to quit. He still did, he thought to himself, and wanted this meeting over with.

"I have a wife now. I don't need the extra stress or hours.

I'm sorry, but I'm not at all interested in taking over Howard's duties or position." Mr. Cooley congratulated him and said he'd not heard that, seemingly ignoring the rest of what he'd said. "We've not tied the actual knot yet, but it's soon. As I said, I don't want the extra stress."

"I can understand that, Dalton, but how much less stressful will it be for you when the town starts having a high crime rate? It will, too. It's been known to get a lot worse with no one in charge." Bad move, he thought. The town would do just fine without him, and he told him that. "I don't think so. I believe, as does my entire department, that it's only been this peaceful here because there are good cops in charge. And failing that…well, I hate to say this to you on such an occasion, but we'll have to find someone else to be in charge that'll be willing to help us out when we need it. If it's not you, then we'll have to find someone that will do it."

"That sounds like a threat. Are you sure you want to go that route? I mean, are you saying that if I don't take this position, you're going to fire me?" Mr. Cooley only smiled. And Dalton had a thought. He really was threatening him. When Dalton stood up and put out his hand, so did the man. "Well, I'm really glad that you came by today. It was very nice to meet you."

"You as well, Dalton. You're a good man. So, if you could just sign off on these contracts, I'll be on my way. You can expect your first pay raise in about a month. I know that seems like a long time, but you know—"

"I'm not going to sign any paperwork, Mr. Cooley. Thanks, but no thanks. As I stated several times now, I don't want to be in charge. Ever. I'm not even sure that I want to be a cop anymore. You giving me an ultimatum did the trick in my decision. So thank you for that." Cooley told him that he'd not be able to do the job without a contract. "Exactly.

But I do want to thank you for coming by. Like I said earlier, I don't have a lot of time now to be sheriff. I thought I'd be able to work as just a cop, a good one, as you pointed out, but I can see that's not going to work now. I just don't care to be threatened."

"Wait. Now wait a minute here. I didn't threaten you." Dalton didn't say anything. "You have to take this job, Dalton. We need you to be in place, or we'll have to look for someone else. Do you have any idea how long...? Look, I'll rush your raise through today, and make sure you're paid for the time you've been acting sheriff too."

"No thanks." Dalton made his way to the door, feeling better and better with each step he took. He felt lighter with the decision as well. "Now, I do have some retirement coming, and a few other company made investments, but I can have my attorney look those over for—"

"I don't think you and I are on the same page here." Dalton told him he thought they were. "No. You see, you think I was threatening you. And I can understand how that would make you feel, but I didn't mean to come across like that. No, not at all. Perhaps we can sit back down and start over, man to man."

"No." He saw Vance coming up to the front steps, and before he could knock on it, Dalton opened the door. "Just a minute, Vance. I have to get this taken care of. This man here, he works for the State Department. He just told me that if I didn't take the sheriff's job that I'd be out of work. I took him up on the deal. I was just asking him to leave when you showed up."

Vance, ever on his feet, said he was glad he'd finally done it, and asked if Dalton needed his help in putting the man out. Dalton, instead of answering him, turned to Mr. Cooley again. The man was still sputtering about money and needing a sheriff.

"I wanted to thank you again for coming by. It was nice to hear how appreciative you were of my work for this town for the last fifteen years. But as I have told you, again and again, I'm going to have a new wife soon, and I don't care to be threatened. Not by you or any other man." Cooley started to speak again, but Vance stretched his neck and the loud popping noise was enough to wake the dead. "My brother and I can show you out should you need any help."

"Dalton, surely you're not turning this position down. It's what you were born to do." Dalton told him it was too late to back track now. "I'm going to call you in a few days. When I do we're going to just forget this conversation happened."

"I already have." Stepping out onto the porch was wonderful. They watched as the man made his way to his car, and he and Vance sat down on the new porch swing as the man drove off. Vance said nothing for several minutes as he sat with him, and it wasn't until Cooley was out of sight for ten minutes that he spoke.

"I'm assuming from that little conversation that I heard that you've just quit your job." Dalton nodded. "I'm also sensing, and this just could be me, that you're not unhappy about this whole chain of events either."

"No, not in the least. I feel pretty good. I think this has been a long time in coming." The swing began to go back and forth, and Dalton watched the tree line get larger then small as they moved. It was relaxing, actually, and he felt his body start to mellow out with the motion. "I should have discussed this with Gabriela first, I think. But I had no idea he was coming here, or that I'd need this so badly, until he did."

"Sometimes that's all it takes, a little push." Dalton nodded and asked him how he was doing. "Good. Much better than before. I think, as I told Gabe, that I wasn't healing as quickly as I had before this simply because there were so many wounds. Good to know, I think. Also, I wanted to talk to you about the latest magic. I can...I think I can hear dragons."

"Me too. And if you need them, there are two that will just suddenly appear out of nowhere to help. They don't seem to respond to simply calling them to see if you can, but only if you need them. Gabriela figured that out." They rocked some more. "I've been thinking about you a lot lately. I have two questions for you. You don't really have to answer either of them. I believe that I have them. The answers, I mean."

"Go ahead. But I reserve the right to not answer you." Dalton said that was fine. "Also, now that you don't have the police hanging on your every word, I'd like it if you were to help me out with the cigarette bust. I just need a man to keep me from being shot to fuck when I head in there."

"I can do that. No problem. First question." He rocked a few times, thinking how best to ask. "About five days ago, I read this article about an elite team of men that went in a country that barely has a government, and got a hostage out and home. There was no mention of names, nor the country they might have been working for. It was a success, I'm to understand."

"Yes, it was." It wasn't a question that he wanted to ask, but he felt he'd gotten all he was going to get from Vance. It was more of a...an agreement of sorts. "You have a second question, then ask. I have to be somewhere in two hours."

Dalton looked at his brother. He had noticed when he was laid up in his house after being shot that he was looking exhausted. There were marks on his body as well, scars like one would have from a knife fight. Bullet holes, more than the ones that he'd gotten that day. And he was pretty sure that Vance would have more by now too.

"How deep are you, Vance?" He would understand what

he was asking him. How deep undercover was his operation. There wasn't any doubt to him that his brother worked for people who not only had no names, but also worked for an establishment that simply referred to themselves by initials.

"I'll never see the light of day again." Dalton was afraid then. Not for himself but for Vance as they sat there rocking like they had not a care in the world. "Grady knows. Everything, I think. Harper too, I guess. They have that mind thing going on, and I'm sure they looked. But don't…if it comes to you, don't go looking."

"I'd like to help you." They rocked, the swing not just moving now but seeming to be cradling them in some sort of temporary bliss. "Vance, I'd like to help you out of this. I don't know what it might be, but I can help you."

"Would you be willing to kill me, Dalton? I mean, not just put a bullet in my head, but to remove it from my shoulders and leave me there?" Dalton told him no. But he wasn't sure that he heard him. "I've thought of nothing else over the last months. To end it all…it's too much anymore. The crimes are harder to walk away from. And sometimes, that's about all you can do."

"I'm sorry, Vance. I truly am."

Vance said nothing. The two of them sat there for over an hour, both of them lost in thought. And when his brother spoke again, Dalton felt chills run over his flesh.

"There are men coming for the jewels, more than we could have imagined, and they're deadly. But they're only pawns in all the killings and trouble. There is a man who is manipulating them in a direction he wants them to go to find the jewels for him. Then he'll kill them off…anyone, as a matter of fact, that gets in his way. I do believe that he holds one of the pieces." Dalton started to ask him if he knew who he was when he continued. "One in particular is close, but he's not going to live long enough to collect on them."

"Are you going to kill him before he gets close?" Vance said that he wouldn't have the chance. "Then this person will? The one you were talking about?"

"Yes, unless he gets stupid or brave. I don't know anything about him, this man I've started calling Operator. He's old, like Kurt, but not much more. He's magical—black magic, as a matter of fact—but other than that, nothing." Dalton asked to be informed if he found out anything else. "I will. In the meantime, you should think about becoming a consultant. To the police. You can pick your own hours, take jobs that you want, and pretty much stick it to them when it comes to getting paid a good salary. That man that left here? Cooley? He has a thing going on with his boss right now that is going to hit the fan soon. I'd want to stay as clear of him as you can."

After Vance left, Dalton realized that he wasn't sure why he'd been there. Probably to tell him about the hunters. But then again, with Vance, it was hard to say. As he rocked, wondering about what he was going to do with his time now, he decided to go into town and have some lunch at the diner.

By the time he got to town, the music was blasting so loudly that he wouldn't have heard a bomb go off even if it had been in his car. Dalton was feeling pretty good about life in general. Pulling into the parking lot, he had completely forgotten about Gerald being out for a couple of days. But as soon as he exited his car, he saw the man sitting in the diner with Milly. He was invited in as soon as they saw him.

If every day was like this, Dalton thought he could surely enjoy being a man of leisure. Yes, it was great working, but he deserved this, even if it was only for a few days. Going into the diner, he was greeted with a big hug and a piece of pie. Dalton was glad for both.

~~~

79

"But you don't understand what I'm telling you. I don't want to have to miss work. You know how much that is gonna hurt me?" Gabe told him there was assistance he could get to help with the bills. "Oh, that's not the reason. My wife will be home. I can't be there all day with her. We survived more years married like we have on account'a I go to work every day, and even going in for extra. No, I can't be home 'cause I don't want to be with my wife. She's meaner than a rattlesnake."

It was hard not to laugh. This was only her third patient of the day, and she'd laughed more in that little time than she ever had at her other job. Sitting on the room's chair, she tried to think what she could do to help the elderly man.

"I don't know what to tell you, Mr. Canes. If you don't stay off your foot, you're going to lose it. I think Dr. McCade already told you this." He nodded, telling her how sorry he was that he'd not listened. "Don't be sorry. That's not going to do you squat right now. If you don't stay off your leg and keep it elevated at least five hours a day, then more at night, you'll be spending a great deal of your time with your wife because I'll have to amputate, and that would permanently put you at home."

"You're not nice. Jesus H. Bunker Hill, she'd surely kill me if I had to be there and under her feet, as she calls it, all the time. Scares the bejeebies out of me, it rightly does." He looked down at his leg like it was entirely its fault. "I got me the sugar when I was a little tyke. Back then it was something that killed you off. I was lucky all these years, not having to do much more than just go on about my business. Then I get this here little bitty sore. It was nasty after a bit, then it started to grow. 'Fore I know it, I'm in here talking to Doc Mac, and he tells me that I went and moved down a number. And not like a lotto either, I was in trouble."

"Yes. Type one diabetes, or the sugar as you called it, means that your pancreas isn't working well. You should have been watching what you ate and keeping up with your testing every day. Exercising would have helped a great deal as well. Just a little walk around the neighborhood without stopping for a donut or pastry." He said he knew that, but for as mean as his wife was, she sure could cook. "You'll have to cut out the sweets, Mr. Canes."

The look on his face was priceless. He stared at her like she'd just told him he had to cut off his leg, which might yet happen if he didn't take care of himself. She started to let him know what he could eat for substitutes, but he was still talking about the sweets.

"You're trying to kill me off, ain't you?" She assured him that she only had his best interests at heart. "I don't think you can rightly say that to a man and then tell him he can't have any more pie and cake. Good Jehoshaphat, woman, you raised by the devil himself?"

By the time she'd convinced him that she'd been raised by regular people, Kenton had come in the room. He said that he'd heard that she had Anderson Canes, and wanted to see if he was following his instructions. Which he had not, apparently.

"She done went and told me that I can't be having any of Beth's pie. You know as well as I that people come from other states just to get themselves a slice. Why, last year, she took first prize in the baking contest." Mr. Canes shook his head. "You tell me that she's fibbing to me, Dr. Mac, and I'll be just as happy as that boy with his thumb in the plum."

"Mr. Canes, we've talked about this. I told you that without a proper diet and taking your meds you'd be back in here. Didn't I tell you that?" Mr. Canes nodded and tried to convince them both that his Beth was the best cook in the world, and to deny him that was as good as killing him. "If you'd like, you can tell her to call in here and we'll give her recipes for things that would be good for you."

"Nah, she'd just throw them out. Never used one of them cookbooks either when we first started our family out." He sat there looking so forlorn that she wanted to go find him a donut. "Well, guess I'll have to do something. I can't lose my leg, you know. Have to work, you know. If I have to stay at home, Beth might just double her cooking efforts just to get rid of me. And I won't be able to tell her no. She sure can bake up a storm when she wants to, Doc. You know that."

Kenton closed the door behind Mr. Canes when he left. He was going to give it his best shot, he told them. And he was surely going to take a little walk when he could get himself going. The man was eighty-four years old, Gabe knew, and to have gone this long without any trouble with his sugar, as he called it, was a miracle. Besides, if he had to leave work, a bagger at the local grocery store a couple of days a week, she might begin to shop elsewhere. She was sure that everyone would. The man was a charmer.

Kenton leaned heavily against the door and let out a long breath. Gabe thought he was in trouble. She asked him what was wrong. When he spoke, she was sure he had to be kidding.

"Don't ever, under any circumstances, ever, eat a single thing that comes from the Canes' household. I mean, not even if you're starved and that will be the only thing between you and death." She asked him about the award she'd won. "Everyone is afraid of her. Terrified, really. She enters the cooking contests every year. And when the judges see that she's made something, rather than having to taste, they declare her the winner. And not a single person protests. Of course, they do award the ribbons to the rightful owners later, but not in front of her. I'm telling you, Gabe, she's really a horrific cook. Don't eat her cooking. Ever. And the peanut brittle that she sends here at Christmas? Well, brittle takes on a whole new meaning when you try to bite into it." Gabe was still laughing when Kenton shivered, his face looking like Beth could be lurking around the corner with a bag of the dreaded stuff. And when he left her to go to his next patient, she sat at her desk and just shook her head. It was a real joy working here.

By lunch she'd seen two more patients and a cat. It took her a few moments to realize it was just a cat, but once she did, taking care of Billy Cannon's kitten was easy. Rural doctoring wasn't nearly as stressful as it had been at the big city hospital. She was glad to see Gavin in the waiting room when she passed by there on the way to getting her jacket. Gabe asked him what he was doing there.

"Nothing. I just came by to offer you a date for lunch. Mom is on a buying trip today, and Aunt Emma went along for support. I think they both just love getting out of the house now." She said she'd love to have a meal with him. "Good, I brought it."

Kenton joined them for lunch. As they sat there she noticed that Gavin kept watching the clock. It was on the tip of her tongue to ask him about a date when he looked right at her and smiled.

"What's up?" He flushed bright red. "Okay, now I know something is up. What is it, and why did you not tell me right away what it was?"

"I didn't want you to be mad at Uncle Dalton." She asked him how she'd be mad. "I can't tell you. It's not bad, I promise you, but he needed this."

"He finally quit." Gavin nodded at Kenton. "Hot damn. I can't believe he finally did it. Dalton has been threatening to do just that for years."

"Dalton quit his job as a cop?" Kenton told her about how he'd been watching the offices since his friend and boss had died. "I thought he enjoyed being an officer of the law."

"He did for a long time. But after a while, like most jobs, he got sick of it. Mostly the way people treat each other. How he had to go in and take care of every little thing in the offices as well. Dalton told me once that he spent more time doing paperwork that was just a repeat of the same information on every page than he did actually walking the streets." She nodded, wondering why he'd not spoken to her about it, then realized that it really wasn't any of her business. They were lovers, not married. "You can't be mad at him for this. Please?"

"Good heavens no. I think he should do whatever makes him happy. And I'd have no room to talk anyway. I quit my job as well." She sat there eating chips and peanut butter sandwiches, thinking. "What do you think he'd like to do now? Not that he should hurry into things, but I wonder what it would be. I love being a doctor. More so now that I'm here. I love this town and the people."

"Short order cook." Gabe looked at Kenton. "I'm serious. He did it for a while going to the academy to earn some extra cash. Then when he got out, he worked with Gerald at the diner for a little while until a position on the force came open. He loved it, everyone could tell. And while he isn't nearly the caliber that Lewis or my wife is, he can make the fluffiest pancakes you've ever eaten."

"He's been cooking for us...." She looked over at Gavin. "You brought us lunch. We didn't go to the diner, when I know for a fact they were going to open today. Yet here we sit having lunch. He's there now, isn't he? Flipping burgers and pancakes."

"I didn't want you to be mad at him." She stood up and Gavin did as well. "Are you going to go there now?"

"Yes, I have a hankering for a burger and fries. Anyone want to join me?" They were walking to the diner when something else occurred to her. Kenton was protecting his brother from her. She looked at him. "Did you know this? About Dalton going to work at the diner?"

"No, I didn't. I'm glad he is, but I didn't know." He took a few steps, then turned to look at her. "You think I knew and didn't tell you?"

"I thought you were protecting him. I don't know why, but I thought you were keeping it from me so I'd not stop him." Kenton shook his head. "I won't hurt him. Never. I want him to be happy. Like I am."

"He might not have done it had you been with him." She asked him why. "Because quitting his job had to be the hardest thing he's ever done, but was much needed. Had you been there, he *might* have quit, but I don't think so. You would have been front in center in his mind. And though I'm pretty sure that you could both make it on your income alone, he wouldn't have seen it that way. He would have needed, and I do mean needed, to support you. It was perfect timing, but maybe he wouldn't have gone to the diner yet. It was time for that as well. Dalton isn't one for taking chances. And I'm betting now that he has you in his life, he'll take even less."

"I don't want him to do that. To change his life around just because he has me in it. If that's what this thing between us is, permanent, I want us both to be happy." Kenton told her that was the way things went. "So you're telling me to suck it up and roll with it?"

"I'd never say something like that to a woman. Not one that I work with anyway. But yeah, that's what I'm saying." She told him she didn't like him. "You know? I get that a lot."

When he opened the door to the diner for her and Gavin, who was laughing at them, she looked at Kenton. "You love him. And I know that. Right now, I'm not sure what I feel, but I want nothing more for him than to be as happy as he can be."

"I know that. And if it makes you feel any better, I think Dalton is happy. In fact, I know that he is. You're the reason for it. He needed you in his life to balance him. As I do my Emma." She nodded, and just before she turned to go inside, she hugged him, and was glad when he returned it. "I sort of kind of like you too, Gabe."

"I like you too, but don't let it go to your head, big guy. I can still hurt you."

They were both laughing when they entered the very crowded diner. Gabe was glad to see the entire town seemed to be out supporting their dragon.

CHAPTER 7

Dennis Howe hated small towns. They didn't have the money that would support a large hospital, and if he had to be in a small town for more than a couple of days, he always made sure there was a helicopter pad nearby to have him flown out if anything should happen to him. He had no idea why on earth Dr. Nola — Gabriela — had come to this little hick town. But he was going to do everything within his power to get her to go back with him. She just didn't understand what she was doing to him...to his hospital by leaving the way she had.

His appointment with her was at ten. Making an appointment like he was a patient was beneath him, but it was the only way he could see her. No one in this little town would tell him where she was staying. There wasn't any listing for her in the phone book. And he was pretty sure that even had he called her, she wouldn't have seen him. No, he thought, this was the best way possible to talk to her.

Dennis could have had any time he wished to see her. Gabe had a lot of openings today, the nurse told him. That alone showed him, and should her as well, that he was right in telling her she needed to return to the hospital. Early was good. He thought if he could get in and convince to return with him, he'd have to spend as little time as possible here.

When his name was called, he went to the reception desk. That was all it was too, a desk. Not a fancy window that slid back and forth, but a big antique looking desk that had pictures and flowers on it. Dennis thought it was the most unprofessional thing he'd ever seen.

Then there was the décor of the office itself. It looked as if someone had gone to a flea market and bought every tacky thing they could find. There were old tin signs on the walls that touted elixirs. One whole wall was dedicated to framed bottles of old medicines. Some of them were items that his hospital hadn't used for decades. There just wasn't any profit in them any longer.

The furniture didn't match anything. Large overstuffed chairs sat alongside of something his mom would have called pressed back kitchen chairs. A large old trunk in the corner overflowed with toys and games. A ladder was leaning against one of the walls with hanging magazines over each of the rungs. Dennis thought that this McCade person should be horsewhipped for having so little care about how he projected himself in this office.

Then there was the building itself. It was in a large warehouse in which someone had divided up the rooms to make it look homey, he supposed. He could see the profit in it. There would be at least two dozen rooms beyond here, he'd bet. A doctor could see as many as twenty patients an hour with all the room, and really turn a good profit if they'd only clean up the front area. That was the smartest move anyone could have made, he supposed. Get a lot in, spend no more than three minutes with each person, then move on. Yes, that was wise on the owner's part. But for some reason, Dennis was sure that the doctor took his time, five minutes with each person, before moving on, cutting his profit in half. Stupid hick.

He smiled now at the woman who sat at the desk, handing her the paperwork that he'd not filled out. "I just want to have a conversation with Dr. Nola. I don't need to see her as a patient. I told you this an hour ago when I got here."

"You sure did." She stood up and Dennis took a step back. He'd not realized how tall or large she was. "But I also told you to fill it out so I can get a record of your visit. Now, you wanna see Dr. McCade, then you fill this out right—"

"Dr. Nola. Gabe, I want to see.... Christ, am I at the wrong clinic? How many of them are there in his stupid town?" She growled, actually growled at him. And when she shoved the clipboard with the broken pen attached at him, he had no choice but to take it. "I need to see Dr. Nola."

"You said that. And as soon as you fill out that paperwork, like I've told you several times now, then you can go on back and see her. And so you know, there ain't but one clinic in this town, and Dr. Nola is no longer Nola. She got herself a man."

Dennis sat. She found herself a man? What the fuck did that mean? He looked down at the form in front of him and started filling in the blanks while his mind worked out the problem it was going to be with her having a man, and what that would mean to him. He surmised that was what the woman meant when she said that Gabe had a man, since she was now going by McCade. How the hell had that happened so fucking fast?

When he was finished, he took the clipboard to the desk. He wanted to tell the woman that he didn't appreciate her attitude or her tone with him, but he said nothing. She might make him sit there longer, and he really did want to get out of there.

"I'll take you right back, Mr. Howe." Nodding, still biting his tongue, he was nearly run down by a little boy. The kid just smiled as he moved past him and into one of the many rooms. "Don't mind him. His momma just got a job, and we're keeping an eye on him today."

"You run a daycare center here as well?" She just glared at him. "How is this place even staying in business? Do you have any idea what sort of standards you're violating?"

"There are standards and there are standards. We like our little place here, and besides, Jeremy there needs someone like us watching over him on account'a he has a cold. Snotty nose and all. I sure do hope you don't get it. It'll have you draining from every hole you got on your face."

She was still laughing at him when she showed him in the room. As soon as she shut the door he went to the little sink and began washing his hands. That was all he needed, to be sick.

Sitting in the large wingback chair, he realized that he'd been wrong about the patients' rooms. They were entirely too large. This one looked to be the size of his bedroom at the breakfast place he was staying tonight. When he did a quick calculation in his head, he thought there could only be about five rooms behind the desk, and that would seriously cut back on their profit margin. Dennis was going to write up a little report for the owner when he left, as a gift for taking Dr. Nola...McCade back with him.

When she came into the room with him, he could tell that she was upset. He'd be that way too if he had to work here, or even had to stay in this town. Dennis stood up and offered her his hand and his sympathy in all that she'd had to endure.

"You're sorry? For what? You have no idea what you're talking about, Dennis. I've had nothing but a wonderful experience working here. Now, what do you want?" He was flabbergasted by her statement. "Dennis, I have three more patients today, and you're taking time from them. What do you want?"

"Three? It's only just after one. You should have at least...." He did the math in his head quickly. "There should be as many as fifty more people to see today. What are you doing? Spending hours with each person? That won't do… how will you make any money?"

"It's not always about that, Dennis. It's more of the thought of paying that makes this job perfect. Why, just this morning I got paid with a quilt. It's quite beautiful, and I'm excited about putting it on my bed. Yesterday a woman brought me eggs and home-cured bacon. We're having that for dinner tonight, with some homemade biscuits." He was shocked that she'd fallen so far beyond what he wanted for her. "I want you to tell me what you're doing here."

"I've come here to take you back to work. I can't believe I have to say this to you, but Gabe, you've really fallen in with the wrong group. I'm betting that you're not getting paid as much as you were making working for my hospital. Nor, and this is quite obvious, nor are you as happy as you think you are. Bacon and quilts? How the hell do you expect to make any sort of profit if you're taking goods over money to pay bills? What do you do about prescriptions? Do you call in some voodoo witch to chant over them, and then let her have a chicken?"

"Don't be obtuse. Of course we can't use the witch. She's on her honeymoon with the local troll." He wondered if she was joking, but she continued before he could ask. "Actually, I'm so happy I could just about bust. And I am making more money for the simple reason that I don't have to kill myself every day to pick up the slack of other doctors who don't show up." She went to the little refrigerator and pulled out a bottle of water. After offering him one, she sat down. "I'm not overworked or stressed out, and I have time to have a nice lunch. Today I had a juicy hamburger with fries that my husband made me. He's a grill cook at the local diner. And you know what was the best part? I got to eat the entire thing and not have to wolf it down like an animal so that I could hurry back to work. It was wonderful. It was liberating."

"Husband? You can't be serious. People like you don't marry. And doctors do not marry grill cooks. What have they been giving you? Drugs?" She stood up and Dennis pushed her back down. "Look. I'll book us a flight out of here and we'll set you up in a nice hotel for a few days, to make sure that kid out there didn't give you something. That's all it is, more than likely, you have a fevered brain. Then after that, I'll put you on the schedule and you'll get back to the way things were before. I'm telling you, when you gave your notice I thought for sure you'd be back by now. And this time you're going to have a nice contract with no loopholes in it. That one you had your attorney fix up was really bad of you. It allowed you things that I never thought you'd follow through on. Well, it's all water under the bridge now and taken care of. You leaving like you did wasn't very professional of you."

"I gave my notice, Dennis. And I worked it out to the end. It's not my fault that you couldn't get anyone to replace me. I'm not going anywhere with you." He told her that he'd not even tried to find her replacement. "Then that's your loss. As I said, I'm not going back to work for you."

She stood up and he pushed her back down again. He had no idea where she thought she was going, but he wasn't finished. But before he could launch into another reason she had to return with him, she hit him, knocking him back into the chair across from her and bloodying his nose.

"What the fuck did you do that for?" She told him she wasn't going to be pushed around. "You were leaving and I'm not finished speaking yet. What brought that on? I'll expect you to apologize to me right now. That isn't any way to treat your boss, Gabe."

"You aren't my boss and never will be again. I told you when I left I was finished. I'm working here now and I love it." He took the tissues when she handed them to him. "I think you need to leave, Dennis. I don't even know why you came here. Or how you got it in your head that I was going to go anywhere with you."

"I think you're thinking of this all wrong, Gabe. You can't be happy here, married to some cook. What the hell were you thinking marrying anyway? You know as well as I do that he's going to expect you to support him. And what sort of money could you be making here to afford that? No, you're not seeing this right. I'll just make the arrangements and you'll come back with me."

"No." He let out a long breath. This wasn't going the way he wanted it to and he was beginning to get angry. "You need to leave."

"Gabe, you don't know what you're saying." He watched her go to the door and open it. The big man, Kenton, as she called him, came in the room too. Dennis stood up and tried to make himself taller by bouncing on his toes and heels. It wasn't working. Whatever they were feeding these monster sized men around here, it was working. "I was just talking to Gabe here, telling her that she needs to come back with me."

"My sister isn't going anywhere unless she wants to." Dennis looked from her to the man. "Yes, you heard me, she's my sister. As of the moment she and Dalton got together."

"Dalton? The burger flipper?" Kenton nodded. "I see. Your mother must be so proud. A doctor and a burger flipper. What else is in the family? A child molester?"

He should have seen it coming. Dennis knew he'd gone too far with the comment about the molester. But he'd been trying to make a point. The fist to his face, he supposed, was the good doctor's way of making his point. Dennis felt his head explode in pain. And then nothing.

~~~

Dalton laughed every time he looked at the unconscious man on the gurney. He had both his eyes blackened, his nose was obviously broken, and he was going to need stitches to put his lips back in the right place. He wondered what would have happened to his poor face had Gabe not been there to pull Kenton off the man.

"You think he'll press charges?" Dalton told the cop it was clearly self-defense. "How did you come up with that one?"

Dalton was there as a civilian, but it didn't mean that he wasn't concerned with the law. Not that the other police were treating him that way, more like he was lead man on the case, but he pointed to the overhead cameras in the office where the man had been.

"My wife said that he pushed her a couple of times too when she tried to leave the office. I guess that he gave Sharon a hard time as well." The cop, Billy was his name, looked shocked. No one messed with Sharon and got away with it. "This man has been brewing trouble since he arrived late last night."

"I'll take him to the cell then. You coming by to talk to him later?" Dalton reminded him again that he was no longer employed as a cop. "Yeah, you said that, but we all think of you as one of us still. You come on and talk to him later, and we'll make sure that the cameras are off in there, if you know what I mean."

"I do, and you'll do no such thing. That'll get all of us in trouble if you try something like that."

The cop nodded and walked away. Christ, what the hell was wrong with people nowadays? Dalton went to find

Kenton and Gabe. They were in Kenton's office going over the event with another officer.

"Do you think he'll leave now? Without taking me with him?" Dalton told Gabe that he doubted it. "Yeah, more than likely not. He seems to think that I've really lowered myself by marrying a burger flipper."

"It was when he insulted Mom that got me. To think she'd be ashamed of any of us for doing what we want." Dalton sat down as Kenton continued. "I have to say, I was really surprised when you showed up. I thought for sure you were going to shift into your dragon and kill him. Christ, I don't think we could take another clean up like we had with Emma's mother. That was a mess."

"It was."

As Kenton explained to Gabe about the men who had come in to kill Emma and her mother pretending to be dead, Dalton thought about his new job. He really did like it, and he hadn't felt this good in a very long time. Looking up when Kenton said his name, he realized that his beautiful mate was nowhere to be seen.

"I asked her to take a patient of mine for me. I wanted to talk to you." Dalton nodded and asked him what was up. "Have you spoken to Vance lately? I mean, I noticed that his house was being worked on. I wondered if you knew anything about that."

"No, I know that Kurt is watching over things for him, and that Opal has finally moved in with Kurt because of something that Vance said to her. I don't know what it might have been, but it must have worked." He told him about the cigarettes in the warehouse, but nothing about him being hurt. "What's going on?"

"I got an email from him earlier this morning. You know how he can be when it comes to speaking, his emails are pretty much the same. But all it says is, 'The next one is coming.'" Dalton asked if he meant the next woman. "Yes, and I have a feeling that he's not going to come home until we can figure out if this person is Lewis's mate or not. It would be like him to do something like that."

"Pretty much. I did point out once, a while back, that we'd all have to be mated to bring this thing to fruition, and he snorted at me. I think he believes there is no one out there for him. I mean, he is a little intense." Kenton just rolled his eyes. "I guess we'll have to get things ready here too. Be better prepared. I'm really surprised that no one has come for Gabe." Dalton thought of the conversation he'd had with Vance, and his promise not to tell anyone most of it. "Grady knows where the next pieces are, right? And I know that we all agreed that we'd be better off just making sure that they're all right and not go to them. I get that. But what if Vance is out there watching over one of them now? I mean, that could be what he's about, couldn't it?"

"I guess. I think we should have paid more attention to Vance when he was younger. He's gotten away from us." No shit, Dalton thought, but said nothing. "You think he's all right? I mean, we've all said that he looks really burnt out. I don't want him to think that just because he's not here, that we don't worry about him anyway."

"I think, and you know as well as I do, that Vance does what he wants. But I think that if he needed us, he'd come for help. He might be really stressed and this badassed guy, but I will never believe that he's stupid. Do you?" Kenton shook his head, but he didn't look sure. Dalton thought he'd ease his mind. "He asked me to help him with this cigarette bust soon. I don't know what he wants me to do, but I jumped at the chance to help him. And since I'm not a cop anymore, I mean officially someone that has to follow the rules, I think we'll work well together. Don't you?"

"Yes, I do. And I'm glad you're going to be helping him out. I just wish he'd come home to us. For good."

Dalton said nothing. He wasn't sure that Vance would be able to settle down. Vance was sort of...he was militarized, he thought. Too much death and destruction to have him ever be anything but a hard core killer.

Their mom showed up about an hour later and told them that she had a date with Gabe. They were going shopping for wedding things. Dalton was glad that he had to work the evening shift. He did not want to have to go to the mall with his mom. He loved her to pieces, but she could shop like it was an event and she was going for the big prize. Just keeping up with her when she walked the place was hard enough, but shopping was worse. She could find a sale better than anyone he knew, and still get a better price than it was marked. Dalton thought about warning Gabe, but decided that she was on her own with this one. Laughing, he made his way back to the diner.

He knew something had to be done about the station house. There wasn't really anyone there equipped to handle the daily in and out of things. A schedule, he knew, could take hours, what with all the part timers working for the city. And now that it was coming up on the holidays, he knew for a fact it would be a nightmare. When he'd gone in yesterday to pick up his few things, he'd told them that he was done when asked if he could come and cover.

"I was told flat out that if I didn't take the commander job then I wasn't going to be thought of as a cop any longer. I was, plainly put, threatened." Two of the men he'd worked with for years told him how rotten that was of them. "Well, it could be, I guess. But to be honest with you, I'm sort of happy. I can spend time with my family, and that's something that I've not had a lot of time to do lately. And with a new wife soon, I'll have the energy to keep up with her. Then sometime down the road, I can be a house dad and have a lot more fun than filling out paperwork all the time."

"You enjoy them while you can, Dalton. Too soon they're all gone, and then you got nobody." He nodded at Walter, the oldest cop they had working there. "I miss old Harold, I do, and you too, but if I could do it, I'd be gone from here. I have three kids living with me again and they're not working. Hard life having to re-raise your kids. And their kids too."

Dalton knew that Walter's kids were taking advantage of the elderly man. They'd been offered employment, working for his family or the pack doing construction jobs and such. But each of them had said that it was beneath them to be working menial jobs. He'd have Kenton talk to them. That would put a fire under their asses.

The diner was busy when he arrived. Just as he was setting up to watch what Gerald did for the night shift meals he felt the touch of one of his family. He held onto the table when his mom spoke.

I'm to tell you that I'm all right and so are the rest of us. He told her that was good. *Yes, you bet it is. But I think you need to come here to talk to poor Gabe. She's having a hard time right at the moment.*

What happened? His mom hesitated and he moved to the main part of the diner to talk to Milly. *Mom, I'm starting to freak out a bit, so tell me or I'm going to come there hell bent on leather.*

A man approached us and started talking to Jasmine about her earrings. I didn't think a thing about it, just so you know, but Emma backed away from him. He told Milly that someone had been hurt and she told him to go. *I should have listened to her. Had I done that then....*

His mom was crying. Dalton felt it with his whole heart. Whatever had happened, it was too much for her. Just as he was coming out of the diner, he saw Kenton getting in his car and decided that he'd ride with him. Jorden and Grady joined them before they could leave. Dalton told them what he knew.

Mom, what happened? They could all hear Kenton asking her…it was the family link, he called it, and it would be much faster this way than her telling him then him repeating it to the others. *We're on our way, but you have to tell us what we're coming up on.*

He's dead. Dalton felt his skin crawl and knew it was his dragon. *I don't think she meant to kill him…I know that…but he grabbed me and tried to get the others to listen. Once he wouldn't listen, Gabe killed him.*

Was he one of the dragon slayers, Mom? She said that she had no idea why, but she thought it was simply a robbery. That he'd tried his best to take her purse and her. *And did he have a weapon?*

Yes. She sobbed again. *He had it right at my head, like he was going to fire it at any second. I don't care for that feeling, let me tell you. I don't ever want to…. Then Gabe told him that she'd had these lessons, and that if he didn't let me go she was going to hurt him. But he would not listen. Why wouldn't he just do as she asked him? Politely too, I might add. But he had to be all macho, Emma called it, and now he's dead. Just dead.*

We're here now, Mom. Where are you? Mom told them what store they were near and that there was a huge crowd around them. *Don't talk to anyone. We're on our way in now.*

They located the women when they arrived. The security cops seemed to have no idea what they were doing, and the crowd was standing in what Dalton would consider evidence. But the moment that he saw Gabe, Dalton knew that he had to

99

go to her. She looked beaten. As soon as he touched her arm and said her name, she broke down. Dalton picked her up in his arms and held her to his chest as the others made sure that everyone was all right.

CHAPTER 8

Ronny watched the crowd. He'd been watching them for an hour, trying his best to get as much information about them as he could, when this little pisser came out of nowhere and tried to rob them. Who the fuck tried to rob someone in broad daylight in a fucking mall?

The mall cops hadn't any idea what to do, that much was obvious. On top of that, the woman who the kid had tried to rob seemed to have a better handle on things than they did. She was giving orders like she was a cop, not some old broad that had it all. Ronny sat at one of the dining chairs and waited. He was curious to see what happened next.

The men showing up had him moving himself to a table further away from the hoopla. There was something so very still about them, like they had this and a great many other things under control and weren't going to take any shit. And when one of them picked the chick that had done the deed off the floor and held her, Ronny had a sudden premonition that he was going to be fucked when he got to them.

"You should really back off now, if you know what's good for you." Ronny started to turn to the voice and was stopped. He knew that it was either a very strong finger or a gun touching his head. He'd bet anything that it was a large enough gun that he'd never feel it penetrating his skull.

101

ATHI S. BARTON

"Don't go messing things up for yourself. If you turn and see me then I will kill you."

"Who are you?" He told him he was a fan of his. "Really? I had no idea that I'd done something so fan-worthy. Why don't we have a seat and you can tell me about it?"

"Why don't you shut the fuck up and listen to me?" Ronny wanted to run more than he wanted to turn, but he sat where he was when he felt something sharp touch his back. A knife too? Who the fuck was this guy? "The world is so different than it was in my time. I couldn't go out as much as I wanted once people figured out not only who, but what, I was. It prevented me from being social. I don't even care for being out with people, but when you feel you can't, then you want it in the worst kind of way, don't you? But I did find that it wasn't all that special once I did."

"What are you? And why would you say you're a fan of mine? I don't think I've done anything at all that would make people notice me." The man laughed and Ronny felt his balls tighten up in fear. "I haven't done anything wrong."

"You haven't done anything right, either. The fact that you think you deserve to find the jewels leads me to believe that you don't have a working brain cell in your head." He started to turn to confront the man when the gun to the back of his head became painful. But the blade was gone now, and for that he was thankful. "This is just what I mean. I told you not to turn and here you are thinking that's all you want to do. Just sit right there and listen to me. Those women there, they each have a piece, did you know that?"

"Yes, I know what pieces they have too. There is an order, and I've figured it out." He asked him if he was brain dead. "No, I'm not. Why the hell do you ask me a question then tell me something like that? I know a great deal about the legend and what it means for these people. There are some that claim there are dragons. Who the fuck believes there are — ?"

"There is no set order to them, you moronic fuck. And they are dragons. Every last one of them. They get them when they find the pieces that belong to them. The women, they find the pieces, and then they're compelled to bring them to the men, that's how it works. Once there and they're mated, the dragon will get a bit stronger." Ronny asked him if he really believed that there was a dragon. "There is. Trust me. I'm just not sure how he fits in all this. I mean, I know that he's somehow leading them here, but how he's doing it without being seen is beyond me."

Well, that made no sense whatsoever. There were dragons? Sure there were. And they were leading people around… women around so that they'd come here with a piece of his jewelry. This was the stupidest conversation he'd ever had. Even beyond what that old fart at his mother's house had talked about.

"I thought the jewels were to bring riches to the family; I don't remember seeing anything about a dragon being a part of it. And I'm pretty sure that would be something pretty difficult to hide, don't you? Damn. That's some fucked up shit, if you ask me." The man behind him assured him that he'd not asked. "I think you need to do some more research, buddy. The jewels are always found in a specific order. Ring first, then — "

"Why do you think they failed before?" Ronny said nothing. "They didn't just let the jewels come to them, they looked for them. In order, or in an order they had in their heads. There is no order." His voice carried a bit, and two of the men turned and looked in his direction. Ronny started to move on but the man told him to wait. "I have us covered. They see nothing that I don't want them to see."

Ronny didn't move. He no more believed the man behind

him than he did that his momma was going to kick him out of their home. What was she going to do if she did that? He knew that she depended on him for certain things. Like he did go and get her medications the other day. Of course he'd been telling her for days that he would, and when she nagged him again, he'd gone to get them. But he had, damn it.

"I want you to do just what I tell you. And if you can manage to not get yourself killed, I will cut you in on the money that comes to the dragons." Like that was going to happen, and he told the man that. "Then I'll kill you where you sit and you get nothing at all. I have no use for you other than for you to be a distraction to the dragons. You can either come to help me or you die. You might anyway, but this way you have a goal. Think of it as a worm on the end of a hook."

"Why do you think I need a partner? You want to find them as much as I do, right? Well, go ahead, see what you can do. I mean, I've done really well on my own." He asked him how many pieces he had. "I'm in no hurry to get them from these people. Where they are, it's just fine with me. Why try to get what I know is already within my reach?"

"I see. Well, I have one of the pieces. And I will get the rest with or without your help. It's up to you. You come work for me and I'll not kill you. Otherwise, I do hope you have that little mom of yours all set up with any insurance you might have." Ronny asked him what he got out of helping him. As far as Ronny was concerned, his mom could fend for herself. She wasn't nice to him of late. "I said you'd work for me, not with me. And what do you get besides the ability to keep breathing? How about I give you some cash? A great deal of it."

"How much is a great deal? I have expenses, you know." Ronny tried to think what a good amount was in the event this guy asked him. He had no way of judging what he wore to ask for a lot. A man's clothing said a lot about how much a man had, Ronny thought. "You give me two million right now and I'll help you…work for you."

"Done." Then the man laughed. "You could have asked for ten and I would have paid it. Ten million is nothing compared to what I will have when this is done." Ronny started cursing, and when the knife or whatever it was jabbed him in the back again, he wanted to turn and tell the man off. But a leather case suddenly appeared in front of him and Ronny bent to pick it up. "I'll contact you in two days on what you have to do for me. Sit tight and don't be stupid."

Ronny didn't bother looking for the man when the gun and the blade were no longer touching him. He had a feeling that now that he had the man's bag of cash that he'd be killed before he could spend it. Pulling the tab on the zipper to see what lay inside, he fell back on his ass when he saw the stacks of money.

Closing it back up in the event someone tried to take it from him, Ronny moved to a restaurant in the mall. He was seated and ordering a meal before he got the nerve to open the case again. He was sure it was going to be all one dollar bills with fifties on the top. But as soon as he fanned out a few of the wrapped cash bundles, he started laughing. It really was all real money.

He ate his dinner slowly. Ronny wasn't much into eating in fancier places of fine dining, but the steak and baked potato were really good. He kept looking in the bag, testing to make sure that each stack was what it appeared to be all through the meal. By the time he was done eating and dessert was on its way, he had figured out that he'd really hit the jackpot.

Whatever this guy wanted him to do, Ronny was sure that he could get more money from him. Two million was a lot of cash, but there had to be more of it. He was just thinking of what he was going to do with his money when the bill came for his meal. Not even looking at it, he pulled three of the top bills out of his bag and left. It was time to start seriously having some fun.

The first thing he wanted to do was get himself his own place. He deserved it. Then he was going to find the next piece to the jewels. If that guy was telling the truth and he had one, then Ronny thought he should as well. It would go a long way, he knew, toward establishing himself as a game changer. Ronny got himself a paper and headed to the only hotel in town. It was well past time for him to make things happen. To hell with the guy who paid him for sitting around and waiting on him to contact him.

~~~

Gabe sat very still. She'd been asked by Dalton not to make any sudden moves when they'd come out here on the deck, and she was trying her best to do just that. But she was too excited to do it much longer. He was going to shift for her.

"I'm not sure what I'll look like. I don't even know if I can do it." Gabe nodded, knowing that he was stalling. "You might be disappointed."

"I doubt that. Even if you're only as big as the little ones that came to me that day, I'm not going to be disappointed. Not in you, not ever." He kissed her. "Come on then. Just change or whatever it's called."

She should have known he'd not do anything by half measures. Almost as soon as the words left her mouth, there was a large dragon in front of her. And he was as beautiful as she thought he'd be, too. The really strange part was, she wasn't the least bit afraid or worried that he'd hurt her.

"Oh Dalton, he's gorgeous. You're gorgeous. Don't move. I want to take your picture." She picked up her cell phone and started taking pictures as she described him. "Emma said that

106

you'd have blue on you somewhere. You're all blue. Your eyes are as blue as the oceans. I've never seen a blue like the blue of your body, and your scales are opaque. I bet if you were to stand next to a tree or something you'd not even be visible. And you're hot, like oven hot. I can feel it even from here."

I'd like to fly. Would you enjoy coming with me? She told him not this time. *Don't you trust that I won't drop you?*

"It's not that. Okay, maybe just a little. But I want you to be free in this. Your first time shouldn't be with you worrying about me." She sat down and waved him off. "Go. Take to the skies so that I can see you."

His body was made for being upward. As soon as he took to the sky, just moving his wings a few times to be lifted up, she was jealous that she couldn't join him. Be right up there with him when he did the most breathtaking moves, almost as if he'd been born to it. In a way, she supposed, he had been.

He was having fun, she could see that. Gabe knew that he'd be good at his first flight. Dalton was good at everything he did. But seeing him there, high above the house, she was thrilled for him. It was a sight to see, one that she had never thought to see in her lifetime. A dragon in the sky. And as she was watching, two more dragons joined him, then a third. The brothers had come to play, it seemed.

She should have known that the wives would show up as well. And for as much as she'd hated hospital functions before, she loved these women as much as she did anyone. When Aisha joined them as well, Gabe asked if they wanted to stay for dinner.

"Of course. I've already taken it upon myself to help you out as well. What with Dalton cooking all the time now and you working a great deal helping Kenton, I've gone ahead and hired you a cook." Gabe thanked her. "I thought you'd put up a fuss. I'm sort of disappointed, actually."

"No. I knew that we should have one coming in. But like you said, it's been a little hectic around here. Also, if you know of a good housekeeper, that would be great too. I'm a slob when I get home from work." Emma said that she knew a couple of women that were looking for work. "Great. I should have asked sooner. I want to not be exhausted trying to keep up. This house is more than I ever hoped for."

As they watched the men flying—not too high…they didn't want to attract any kind of attention—she thought of something else. She hated to bring it up now, they were so enjoying themselves, but she needed to know.

"The other day, when you were with me in the studio, I pulled your dragon. Have any of you tried to do it again? I mean, I hope I'm not the only one that can do it." Harper said that she'd tried to pull her own, but it didn't move. "It might be because it's yours. I don't know. But we can try now if you want. All I did was just think of them, and there they were."

Emma put out her hand and touched the dragon that was on Harper. She knew that it would rise up to press against her fingers if she touched her, and Gabe thought it was kind of weird that she could also feel its thoughts when she had touched Grady's arm later that day.

"Wait." They all turned to Jasmine. "I want to test this, I really do, but they're flying. Grady is too. What if we pull the little one from him and Grady falls? Or any of them, for that matter?"

Emma snatched her hand back so quickly it was almost comical. "I don't want any one of them hurt. I agree. Until we know what it does, we'll just wait until they land."

After that they talked about the charity ball that was coming up in two weeks while waiting for the men to come join them. It was nice, really, having them all sitting around like old friends, Gabe thought. Aisha lit up when Gabe asked her how things were going, since it was so close to the final days of it. She told her that things were going wonderfully. Gabe, like the other women, could hear the pride in her voice.

"You should see the things we have had donated already. Expensive things too. One of the companies that we contacted donated dinner for four at their restaurant. And Gavin, oh my, he's been such a wonderful help. I think it's the way he can look things up on the computer, but he has given me so many ideas." Gabe told her that if she thought of anything she could do to help out as well, just to let her know. "Oh yes. I need some help with getting the tables set up. If you could help me with that, I'd be ever so grateful. We started out with just about ten tables of ten, and now, with all the new things we're offering, we've exceeded our expectations by nearly four times that amount. I've had to rent a bigger hall and order so much food. It's going to be wonderfully successful. Just in table sales alone, we've made well over a million dollars. We also could use some help with picking some of the other things up. There are companies that have no way of getting some of the heavier things to the hall."

Emma said that she'd get some of the pack to help out. Perhaps, she thought, they could have a nice cookout to kick things off. Aisha thought it was a wonderful idea and started writing things down to remember. Gabe was pretty proud of her. The woman could move mountains if she set her mind to it, she thought.

"I went to one at the hospital a few years ago. It was the most boring night I've ever had," Gabe told them. "There were casino like tables that no one knew how to run. They ended up just closing them down about half way through the night. Some kind of silent auction, but there were only things like scrubs and a gift card to a shoe place. Very lame.

109

The larger auction during dinner was such a flop too. They had such high minimum bids on things that no one wanted to bid. However, I did get a really good deal on a massage package, but I never used it. The place was a dive, and about a week after I tossed the certificate in the trash, the place was raided for drugs." She laughed. "The only good thing about the dinner was the open bar. I think they actually lost money on that. Come to think of it, after that, I heard that the bar was cash only. That could explain why no one went."

"We've had a couple of people say they would donate their time to run the bar. It's cash only, but reasonable. Wine and beer mostly. And soft drinks. We decided that since we had all the water bottles donated too, we'd just give them to people who wanted them." Aisha grinned as she continued. "I think, since most of the people coming are close, we might not have too much in the way of drunks on the road afterwards. And there is the taxi service that is willing to take them home should they become too…too loose, I guess you could call it."

After the men had had enough, they all stood in the yard to see about the dragons, and how to call them forth. They knew that the little dragons wouldn't come out for simply no reason…Gabe had tried calling to one of them when she'd been at home alone one day just to see if she could do it again. But this was different. This was a test. As Grady and Harper were standing side by side, Gabe stood up first.

"I'm actually kind of nervous. What if it comes out thinking that there is trouble and kills us all?" Kenton told her she had a very scary mind. "You won't think so if that thing comes here and burns your ass off."

"Okay, you have a point." Kenton looked at her. "What do we do? I mean, I know you just had to ask for help, but we don't really need it. And like you said, we don't want to become human tartare either. How is it you did it when you needed them?"

She was slightly embarrassed. "I said, 'Come to me, my babies.' I don't know if that worked—"

They were there, the two of them as they had been before. The larger of the two bowed to her, then to Kenton. But for him, he didn't rise. The female flew up and landed on her shoulder.

The dragon wasn't heavy, not like Gabe thought she'd be. Her body was longer than she remembered. But at the time, she'd been more focused on the men trying to kill them than how the dragons looked. It was the strangest thing that she'd ever had happen to her in all her life, to have dragons standing before her.

You have questions? Kenton nodded and asked the dragon to rise. *I cannot, my lord. I must keep my head lower than your knees. Perhaps if you were to sit, then I could stand to talk to you. Even though you have asked me to rise, you are forever my lord, and I cannot show you any disrespect.*

"All right. I can understand that. But should you ever have the need to talk to me about something important, I do hope you will forgo the protocol and just speak to me. I don't want my family to be harmed while I have to get you to stand and tell me." The dragon said that he would do that. "Good. All right, let's settle so we can talk. I'm assuming that since you are speaking to me through our contact, the others can hear you as well?"

I can make it so. Kenton nodded and she knew when the others could hear as well. *But if I need to speak to you alone, sir, then it will be just the two of us.*

When all of them were seated, the female stood between her and Dalton. She never spoke, but did watch the rest of them like she was protecting her Gabe from them. Gabe wasn't sure if she should or not, but she put her hand on the

111

dragon's back and ran her finger down her length to her tail. She jerked her hand back when something pricked her skin.

You have marked us both, my lady. Gabe asked her what she meant. *By sharing your blood with me, we will be better equipped to speak. I belong to no one but you, my mistress.*

"Shouldn't that be Emma?" The female looked at Emma then back at her, asking why her. "I don't know. She's the queen, from what I understand."

Nay, she is not. She is the first mate of the eldest, but the queen is yonder. They all turned to Aisha. *She is the queen of us all, of all dragons.*

"Oh no, I can't be queen. I can't even talk to Caelin. I can't be queen." The female flew to Aisha and bowed her head. Then before anyone could guess her intent, she dug her claws into her arm. The scream from her had them all jumping up. "I'm not hurt. I was…it just startled me. I swear, I'm not hurt at all."

There was a small mark, no bigger than an inch, on her arm. But as they watched it heal over, it changed. The dragons, two of them circling her upper arm, seemed to resemble the black and white symbol of yin and yang.

"What's your name?" The female turned to Emma when she spoke. "Both of you, I'm sure you have them; what are your names? We'd very much like to call you something besides little dragon and big one."

I am Roderick, male to the female dragon holder. My mate, she is Lyna, and the counterpart to the male holder. Grady asked why they were not male to male. *A balance, my lord. There must forever be a balance for dragons. Same with yourself. Female to our males. It is what makes us stronger.*

They went around the circle and introduced themselves, each of them telling the pair their mates as well as the jewelry they had. The dragons seemed to understand how the pieces worked, so they didn't have to explain that part. Dalton told them the ones of the family that were missing.

Vance. Roderick stood up straighter as Dalton nodded. *He is away much. We will talk later, I am sure.*

"All right. How did you know that he was missing and his name?" He told Dalton that Roderick and his mate lived with them, so they could hear all manner of things. "Okay, I guess you do. But you...you know our voices, but not who we are. I get it."

We can hear many things, as I have said, but much is.... It's all very strange to us. It is the first time we have been awakened in more years than I can remember. The lady queen, Prisane, she put us to sleep when the necklace was broken. No one has been able to awaken us since.

No one said a word. The implications of what he was saying, that no one had gotten as far as they had, was terrifying. Gabe had heard the story about the jewels, the queen, and the dragon, but to think that they were the first to come this far...? Well, she felt sorry for all the lost souls before them and all that they had lost.

You wish for us to show you what we can help you with? Gabe explained what they were doing. *You need only to think of us to have us come to your aid. But with Lady Gabriela, we can do more.*

"Why?" She felt her face heat up. "I don't understand why I'm so different than them. I mean, they've been here longer than me. Shouldn't one of them be able to have all of you?"

You have called us first. It is only fair that we should help you more. She understood the reasons, but that didn't mean she had to be happy about it. *Shall we show you?*

"Yes, please. What is it you can do for us?" She watched him nod and knew that he understood that she was as nervous about this as she was excited. She didn't want special treatment, and she was pretty sure he got that too. "When I called you before, you took care of men that were going to kill us. What did you do?"

We killed them. They're dead, as you know, but we also made sure that there was nothing that would come back to haunt you. He looked at Lyna. *I believe that is the correct wording. Am I right?* At her nod, he turned back to Gabe. *We are here for you, and for all McCades.*

"But the others, they can call you?" He said that was also correct. "Good. I'd hate to think that when they need you, they have to go through me. So, if you're ready, you can show us what you can do to help us."

They took to the sky, not far from them, but close enough that they could see them. First Lyna turned red, the trail she was making getting longer and longer as she flew until it became a circle. Then as she turned white hot, Roderick joined her. His red joined her white, the flames merging together to make a beautiful display of color and heat. Gabe had never seen anything so beautiful yet terrifying in her entire life.

"They're heating up. See? They're molten hot." And they were. So much so that they were no longer blending in colors, but white. She supposed as dragons they could get as hot as they wanted, but it was still a sight to behold. "Watch."

Separating, they flew to the tree line, the two of them still as hot as they'd been as a whole. Each of them then hit a tree. They were so hot that they bore right through the trunk of several trees without any more effort than it took them to fly. The trees, smoking from the damage done to them, didn't burn but smoldered slightly. This went on for several seconds. They would fly to the sky, heat up, and then return to the earth to take out even the smallest of the dead fall. The trek to the sky had them turning in the opposite direction; their bodies, Gabe knew, were cooling down

By the time they returned to them, they were still hot, a blue flame now, and cooled even more as they moved their wings back and forth, seemingly reducing their temperature. The trees, amazingly, didn't fall, but she knew that they would soon enough. Gabe was glad to see that they'd not harmed any of the living trees, only the dead.

"Had that been a human, I'm assuming like the men that you took care of at the studio, they would have incinerated." Roderick nodded and bowed again. "You killed them by running through them and they just disappeared. That explains the ash in the room. It wasn't from a vampire, as we assumed, but from their bodies."

We did not want to leave a trace for others to find. And there are others, as I'm sure you are aware of. Kenton nodded. Then he asked what they could do for Gabe. *She must ask us, my lord. I know that you are the ruler here and to all dragons, but as I said, she called upon us. We will serve her and the rest, but she can call on all our powers and share them with the rest of you. But be warned, once you have been given them, there is no way to rid yourself of them. They are as permanent as we are to our hosts.*

Kenton looked at her, giving her permission, she supposed, to do whatever it took to bring whatever powers they had to all of them. While it was a good plan, she did notice that no one bothered to ask what it was they were going to receive. She supposed, in a way, none of them wanted to know. It was too…well, scary.

"I'm thinking, like the rest are I'm sure, that we need all the help we can get. Am I right in assuming that this is going to be helpful and not harm us in any way?" Lyna told her that it would never be painful to the McCade dragons. "All right then. Let's do this. Show them."

Roderick nodded when Lyna turned to him. Then they took to the sky again. They were higher this time, their trails getting hotter as they flew as one. When they began chasing each other faster and faster, she could not make out one from the other. It wasn't long until they seemed to be a blue blur that formed into a circle. Just as she was going to ask what sort of magic that was, they became one.

"Christ." Gabe didn't know who spoke, but she was pretty sure it was exactly the right thing to say at that moment. No one moved as the dragon flew to the ground.

He was much larger than the two single dragons would have been standing side by side. His wings spread out and the heat from him seemed to touch each of them. Then he turned his head and a white hot flame spilled from his mouth, scorching everything for at least the length of a football field. He looked back at her.

My name is Anton; I am here to serve. When we are as one, as you see before you, we are more powerful than any manmade weapon known to your world. You will come before us, my lady? You and your mate? Gabe had no idea why, but she thought that she could trust him not to harm them. *We will not harm you. 'Tis not possible for us to do so. Your life, and those of every McCade for all generations, will come before ours.*

As she got up, taking Dalton's hand in hers when he rose with her, they stood to the other side of the large dragon and waited. He told them once again that they'd never be harmed. When he asked if they were ready, they nodded. Then the flame hit them…and both her and Dalton were engulfed in the white flame of the dragon.

CHAPTER 9

Dalton was sure there were things going on around him. What was being said, he had no idea. But he had to sit there, just thinking calmly, or he would explode. Even to himself that sounded overly dramatic, but right now, he was pretty sure that's what would happen. His head would just explode. He'd just been flamed by a fucking dragon.

My lord? He told Caelin that he wasn't ready to speak just now. *Then I shall. The dragons have marked you and your entire family. You're immortal.*

Dalton started laughing. He stood then and looked at his family, all of them gathered around speaking quietly, and just laughed. It was too much, simply too overwhelming, and the harder he laughed about it, the looks from them got stranger. It wasn't until someone slapped him that he was able to stop. He sat down on the chair and just held his head in his hands. He wasn't entirely sure that Kenton hadn't enjoyed that just a little too much, but he was glad for it all the same.

"Caelin just told me that we're immortal." Kenton sat down across from him and asked why he thought that was funny. Because as far as he was concerned, it wasn't. "I don't know. I guess it was everything. I have a mate that I love dearly. Dragons that come out when we call them. Said dragons can get hot enough to burn through humans and

117

trees, whichever pisses them off the most, I guess. They can change into this monster creature that can get hotter than what I can only assume hell would be like. And I stood in front of this monster dragon and had him blow flames at me. Could be that I'm a little overwhelmed. I don't know. What do you think? Oh, lest I forget, I wasn't harmed by said flames, and my clothing seems to not have gotten any damage from them either."

"If it makes you feel any better, I think you're taking this very well." Dalton snorted as Kenton laughed. It was full of humor, not stress as his might have been. "What else did he tell you about being immortal? Maybe you just heard him wrong."

He did not, my lord. You're all immortal. As will your children be. And theirs after them, forever. They could both hear him, and when both Jorden and Grady joined them, he thought they could as well. *Any children that come to this family, such as Gavin and any others, will also be given this gift. Your mother as well. Though I have a feeling that she is not all that happy with the idea of being around forever.*

"Is there a way to kill us? I mean, immortality is great and all, I guess, but I'm assuming that there is one way that can. I'd very much like to know what it is so I can avoid it in the future. You know, like is being on a train going precisely eighty-three and a half miles an hour and it turns over going to be a part of that equation? Does there have to be seventy-three humans on board, as well as three paranormals? I'm babbling, I think." Caelin told Jorden that there was only one way, but it would never happen. "How can you be certain? I mean, for all you know there could be a person out there that can do it."

I am the only thing that can kill you, my lord. I would have to remove your head, burn both parts of your body, then I would need to bleed upon your remains. As I said, you will never die because I shall never end your life. Dalton sat back in his chair, looking at his brothers. *You have questions?*

"Yes, so many right now that I don't even know where to begin. Immortal to what? Just death, or do we have this new built in thing that keeps us from harm to our bodies as well? You know, the flames that hit us, we didn't even have our clothing burned." Caelin said that nothing would be able to penetrate their flesh, nothing would make them sick, and they would never age. "So we're pretty much indestructible."

I'm not familiar with that word, but if you mean you cannot be destroyed, then yes, that is what I mean.

There were no words to say that would make this.... Dalton wasn't even sure what he wanted at the moment. Answers were there, but he didn't know the questions. To him, this was getting really weird. He looked at Kenton when he said his name.

"Are you paying attention?" Dalton shook his head. "He said that we have to go and find the next two pieces and bring them to us. The mates will follow."

"No." Kenton asked him why not. "Because if we do that, someone will come here watching for any new females coming to the houses, or even to town. What if they have absolutely nothing to do with this other than to be in the wrong place at the wrong time? I don't think I could live with myself if that were to happen. They'll be fair game without the added extras that the jewelry can give them. Think about it. Emma would never have known to hide when she did. Seek out medical attention from your offices, and I'm betting that when the building blew up she was in, had he not been there for her, with the ring, she'd be dead. Her grandfather would have made sure of it. All of them, all the mates to us, they're here simply because the dragon made it safer for them."

119

You are correct, my lord. I had not thought of it that way.

Dalton looked at Grady. He was too calm, too settled for what was going on around them. He asked him what was going on.

"Nothing is wrong, really. The piece, one of them, is close. Not with a female that we can see, but she's near enough that we can feel her and the piece." Dalton asked him how that worked. "Not sure. I can just feel the pull of the magic from it, and from the woman. Not her exactly, but the thing that attracts her to it, I think. Like...when you smell something, good or bad, it triggers a memory. Harper and I can see that memory, though we aren't entirely sure what it means."

Tell me of it, my lord. Then perhaps I can tell you what piece it might be. Dalton watched Grady, thinking he wasn't going to do it. Then Caelin spoke again. *As the six of you get stronger, so do I. I can remember a great many things now, from the beginning of this quest. The lady queen sitting upon my back when the area around the castle needed to be surveyed. Times with young Caelin, her only child. I remember wars that we fought, those also between her husband, the bastard king, and herself.*

"He wasn't a good man, I'm assuming?" Dalton felt the sorrow from Caelin and regretted the question. "I'm sorry, my friend. I know that you must miss her very much."

Nay, 'tis not that. He wasn't a good man, as you have said. Nor a good husband or leader. My lady queen had much to cover for him in his misdeeds and fights. Affairs that he had, some with a not so willing female. It...I think he said it vexed him to think that a woman had any power, especially over him. He thought, him being a male, that all should bow before him and to do as he said, no matter the consequences that would arise from it. The queen, she never gave him his due as he expected her to. She was a force to be reckoned with at times. Much like the mates that are here now. Each of them, in some way, reminds me of her. Jorden asked what had happened to make her leave him. *He thought there no children born from their union. He felt that she had failed him, my lady queen had not delivered him a boy child. Which in fact she had, almost from the first. When Caelin was born, she hid him away with magic so that the king would not corrupt him in any way. He would have too. Made him into his own image. He might well have killed him as well, for I think him to be a good soul, even for one so small.*

"So she hid her child away, and then when the king came to kill her, she broke the jewelry up into smaller pieces and sent it around the world. Why? Did he do something more than just want a child from her?" Kenton looked around when he didn't get an answer right away. "I think I'm not going to like this, am I?"

The day after they were wed, an arranged wedding by their fathers, Prisane, the queen, was found at the bottom of the staircase beaten and bloodied. He had done this, then walked over her broken body to go to his mistress. The king, Butler was his name, he said to all that would listen that she had not satisfied him. That she would not submit to him. I found out later that he wished for her to be strangled while he took her. It was a game for him, and the only way that he could enjoy her. He thought her to be ugly as well. Dalton had heard of things like that. It had a name, but before he could remember what it was, Caelin continued. *Soon after this, she found herself with child. By then the castle was in near ruin, and there was no money in the coffers to make repairs for some time. The staff would no longer work in the household when he was in residence. Many of the female staff had been raped, some even killed, by him. She had to pay large sums of monies to the families of the people who worked their fields just to keep the crops and foodstuffs coming in. The overlords who would have paid her to be in their keep were now refusing to pay. They said that Butler was making demands on even their wives sexually. It was too much for them to bear. After a time, it was apparent that he began selling off the things of the castle when she started locking away the cash and jewels that were brought to her from the dragons. Horses would come up missing. Art also disappeared from the walls. Sculptures that had been in the family for generations were sold off for drink and women.*

Dalton thought of the things that were in his home. Items his mother had given him when he'd moved out. Treasures such as pictures, ornaments that had been his as a child. There were blankets as well, things that past generations had left for them to share. He didn't know what he'd do if someone were to take those things from him. They all turned to Grady when he cleared his throat.

"Harper and I are going to the castle in a few weeks, to see what we can do to have it brought to its former glory. It looks really bad from the photos that a realtor sent us a few days ago." Caelin told Grady that at one time it housed over a thousand people within its walls. "There are no walls left, it looks like. And the castle itself is falling down. I think we might have to start from scratch."

Once the magic is restored to the family you will not have as much work to do. Dalton wondered at that, but Caelin continued with his story. *One night, after many years of hardship, Prisane heard from the magic that Butler had a mistress that was full of child. She was to be the next queen, Butler told the town, and that they were to pay her homage. The town was already taxed too much; they had no more to give, especially not to a woman who would only demand more if they had it. When asked about the current queen, Butler told them that she would fall dead by the next week. The lady queen then set to work to get the household and her son ready.*

Dalton could almost see the man's anger when he found out that not only was the queen gone, but so were the riches that he assumed would be his. Greedy men, ones like this king, were what had made him hate his job, despite all the work he'd done so that everyone was safe. The dragon continued as Dalton felt his heart break for the terrible mess things had come to back then.

We worked through the nights, the queen and the other dragons, when he would be off with the women. Sometimes we would not sleep, just so that we could use magic to save as much as we could. Money was hidden away. Jewels that had been in the family for so long no one knew who it had belonged to first. Paintings too were stashed in places of safe keeping. And at the end, the jewelry that I forged for her was brought to her so that I might enter it to keep me safe for the generations that would follow. Dalton thought of what he was saying. Money? Jewels and paintings? He wondered aloud if they were still around. *Yes, all of it. And once we are all one, the jewels together, then their hiding places will be revealed. The magic that hides them was buried deep within the sparks that made me. You and the other McCades, all that come after this generation, will never have to worry about such a thing again.*

As they sat there, the four brothers, Caelin asked Grady again what his memory of it was. The pull of the piece that was close enough for him and Harper to feel. Dalton had forgotten about it, he was so wrapped up in the story.

"It's hard to describe. It's memories. I can almost see the day that the young son was born. The room that was cut off from the castle so that the king wouldn't find them. Harper said she could feel the labor pains. They weren't as bad as her having the child, but she could feel them." Grady laughed. "It's like we're right there with them when he was born. But this pulls…it's like right there but just beyond them."

That would be the grounds behind the castle. There is a cave there. I used my own magic to make it safe for them should they ever need a reason to run. I think that young Caelin, he hid there until a time when he could be free of his father's wrath. And there is, hidden deep behind it, a room that was to be used for my queen to raise

123

and to play with her son. Dalton wondered how that would be considered close. *I would think, however, that you are only feeling a place that would be like her own sanctuary. Perhaps there is a cave close by, maybe the new miss will be staying in it?*

"There are several caves surrounding the land we live on. One of them…I think it's about ten miles from where Grady and Harper live." Dalton stood up as he continued. "How about we go and look into it? It'll be better than sitting around here waiting for something to happen, don't you think?"

"Not today." They all looked at Jorden. "I'm sorry, but I can't get away right now. We have to leave in the morning for Paris. I have that show that I set up months ago. Harper and Grady are joining us; we're going by the castle to have a look at it. And I have no idea why I think this, but we have to be together to find her. If that's even the best course of action. Like Dalton said, it might be better if we let her come to us. Just to be safe."

Dalton had forgotten about Jorden leaving, what with all the other stuff going on. But they did make a pact, sort of, not to go looking on their own. It was just too dangerous. Even though they were immortal, they might be hurt or lost screwing around in a cave. So it was settled…they'd go look for it, because it was on their land, when the rest of them returned. Dalton hoped the next mate would be all right where she was.

~~~

Ronny wandered around his new home. It wasn't the one that he'd wanted, but it was pretty close. He supposed that he should have taken better care of his cash than to go out and have a couple of parties, but he'd learned his lesson now and he had his house. And it was nicer than his mother's. Which to him, was very important too.

"You don't have any furniture. Don't think you're taking

124

any of mine, Ronny. I'm going to be letting out your room now that you've moved out. So I'll need that." He wanted to tell her they were his things, but he just moved into another room. His mom had insisted on coming with him today, and he had regretted it from the moment that he'd picked her up.

Almost as soon as they'd pulled up, she'd complained about how the yard needed care. That there were too many windows, and who did he think was going to clean them. Then she asked him about how he was going to keep it up, it was too big for just one man. On and on she went, just as if she had any say in what he was doing.

"I purchased a big house so that I could spread out if I wanted." She just shook her head, something he'd just noticed that she did a great deal when he did something he liked and she didn't. "It's my house, Mom. Why can't you be happy for me?"

"I'm happy for you, Ronny. I am. But however do you think you're going to pay for this every month, and the utilities that go with it, by just looking for those pieces of jewelry? You know that they're probably not even real." He told her that they were real, he'd looked it up. "Yes, so you told me. Hundreds of years old and no one has found them yet. But you think you will. No matter what you say to everyone else, Ronald, I know just how dumb you really are."

He hated her for that. For her thinking that he was a fool. That she called him dumb. Ronny knew he was far from that. He knew that she did too, she just wanted to make him mad. Right then and there, he decided not to tell her about the money that he had used to buy the house. As he made his way to the upper floors he thought of the conversation again with the man last night.

Ronny had been at the mall, looking for new sheets for the bed he was thinking of buying. The man didn't poke him

125

with a knife or a gun this time, but there was still something extremely threatening about him.

It bothered him a little too that he hadn't seen the man's face as yet. He did know the voice now. It was dark. A strange way to describe someone's way of talking, but that was just how it made him feel. Like it was something richer than dark chocolate, but there wasn't any sweetness in it. Just the opposite as a matter of fact. He told him to stand still, not to move a single muscle or he'd be dead. Then he gave him orders, like Ronny was nothing more than a slave to his needs.

"Here is what you will do, and if you do it well, then money will come to you again. I will tell you where to go to find out if a piece is real or not, and you'll get it. By any means. I know that you've killed before for this venture. So I figure that you won't be squeamish when you have to murder in the name of riches. And there will be too. More than you can ever spend in your little life." He said that he might need travel money. "You are not getting any more cash until I can tell whether or not you're going to be helpful to me. 'Tis not my problem that you have been a fool."

"I had to buy some things. I told you, I had expenses." Ronny hadn't tried to turn and look at the man this time. He was actually afraid to see him. But the man needed him, and Ronny was going to make sure that he knew that. "If you would just give me the rest of the ten million that you said you would, I could do a lot of looking for you."

The blow to the back of his head hurt. And when he planted his face in the table he'd been standing near, he had to use all the discarded napkins to clean up the blood from his nose. The man was angry, so much so that Ronny was suddenly afraid.

"You'll do as you're told or you'll end up with the rest of the fools that thought they could outsmart a curse. You'll go for the pieces as I tell you. I'm running out of time. They have only the one piece to get other than the one that I have." He heard the man growl low. "You'll be paid enough to get there, stay for a few days, then return. And upon returning, I will give you more cash. That's the only way you're going to get any more until this thing is finished."

After he'd been left there, his nose bleeding still, Ronny wondered what the man would do if he simply said no, that he wasn't going to play by those rules. But he knew if he did that, the man would have no trouble killing him. There was danger around him that said he couldn't care less what Ronny wanted.

So tomorrow he was going to go to the airport, pick up an envelope from a locker, and take this trip. He had no idea where he was going or how long he'd be gone, nor did he have any idea what he was supposed to be looking for. The man had also told him he had the jewelry all fucked up too. There was still a single piece out there that Ronny thought the family had.

He entered the area that he'd called the jewel room. Ronny had taken all his notes down when he'd been packing at his mom's house, and carefully numbered them so that they'd be hung in the right order. Ronny had so much more space in this house that he had spread out his worksheets to go all the way around the empty room. And there were enough blank pages now that he could add notes as he went. He stood at one of them now, with the things that had been told to him from the Dark Man. That's what he'd been calling him, Dark Man.

"What is all this?" He looked at his mom when she joined him in the jewel room. "Oh Ronald, please tell me that you're not going to continue this. You have to find a real job. That pays you actual money. You aren't moving back in with me, not when the bank takes this all from you. Or if the government takes it for nonpayment of taxes."

"I'm not going to lose anything. I told you, this will be a huge payoff. Why must you always be so negative when you speak to me?" She just shook her head and walked around his room. "I've got a partner now. He's really helping me out in getting closer to the end of this. You'll see, Mom, I'm going to be famous one day soon for finding what others couldn't. People are going to be talking about me for decades, see if they don't."

"Sure they will, Ronny. Famous for losing it all because you didn't know how to take care that you had a job." She was forever harping on him about a job. He did have one, he told her. "No, you have a hobby. And one that is going to have you lose this nice home."

"You think I have a nice home?" She nodded and patted him on the cheek, just a little too hard. But he was willing to forgive her for that if she said it again. "You should see the other rooms, Mom. The master suite is bigger than your living room and kitchen combined. Come on, let me show you."

"I can't today, Ronny. I have to get back and start supper for the live-ins. They wouldn't like to be put off just because my son has a house that is too large for him."

He watched her walk away, heard her going down the stairs. "I wish I could shove you down the stairs and break your neck." He shivered when he thought of how easy that would be, but just let out a long breath. If he could kill her, which he wasn't saying that he couldn't, he knew that it would be something that made her suffer. As she had done to him all his life.

Going out to his car, another new thing he'd purchased, Ronny thought of what he was going to do tomorrow. He was supposed to kill someone. While he was only a little nervous

128

about that part, he was really excited about having another piece of the set. Ronny was thinking of ways that he could keep it for himself, but since the man had sent him for it, he wasn't sure how to make that work. Other than just lying to him.

Ronny thought of all the things he was going to purchase when he got his next allotment of money as he drove his mom home. It would be a nice payoff too. And he was going to be much better at how he spent it. No more parties where he invited everyone. And there wasn't any need for him to buy a second house. Unless it was in another country. That would be nice.

There were men that he knew of that could make a replica of about anything. It had been his plan to have a piece made that looked just like the one he picked up. That was until he found out how much it would cost. Even fake shit took money. But he'd figure out something. He was a smart man, regardless of what his mother said about him.

One guy wanted nearly ten grand just to consider it. Another told him that it would be five thousand, but he wanted to make another for himself. He didn't even care what it looked like, but he collected old things and sold them off cheap. That wouldn't do, not for this project. There were too many people out there, he told him, who were looking for it.

From the looks of his house, he really had been a collector, of everything. Mostly trash, as far as Ronny was concerned. And he had a real fetish for things cut with a chainsaw and made into animals. Bears mostly, but they were everywhere. They parted ways even before Ronny could show him the piece he thought he might be looking for.

Ronny dropped his mom off at her home and made his way into town. He'd been there before a couple of times, but now that he had a house here, close to the McCade family, he wanted to get to know the area. He'd read somewhere that little towns that had diners were great for getting information. They knew everything about everyone. He was hoping for a nice meal and some good gossip when he parked in front and headed inside.

The waitress, Milly her name tag said, asked him what he wanted to drink as she handed him the menu. After ordering tea, he opened it up to look. There were three entries on the thing; breakfast, lunch, or dinner. Ronny flipped it over to see if this had been a mistake. He asked her about it when she returned.

"Nope, you get to pick what you want off there and I'll tell Cook. He's not into making up a list." He asked her what there was to choose from. "Breakfast, lunch, or dinner. We don't have nothing fancy."

"Okay, so do I get like meatloaf or roast for dinner?" She just stared at him. "How about side dishes. What are they?"

"Those are the things that you get with your main course. Haven't you ever been out to eat before?" He told her he had, plenty of times. "Sure couldn't tell. Now, you tell me which meal you want and I'll have Cook make it for you. Them sides you was asking about, they'll come with whichever meal you order. On the side of your plate, or if he's feeling really good, on another whole plate."

Ronny told her to bring him dinner. It was nearly six now, so the timing was right. However, since he had no idea what he might get as his dinner, he just sat back and watched what the other people were eating.

He noticed that there was some work going on in the little place. He saw tape, bright pink, around a place where a table had been, he was sure. A couple of boxes in the corner had Bench Seat printed on them. Ronny thought they were for the diner, or perhaps knowing this place, for a car somewhere that needed them. This entire town was really fucked up.

A man at the counter was bent over his meal, so Ronny had no way of knowing what he'd gotten. The coffee smelled really good, and he decided that if he did get a good meal out of this, he might have some pie and coffee too. He didn't remember seeing it on the menu, but he could smell coconut or something like it around.

When someone sat across from him, he started to object when the man laid a prettily wrapped box on the table.

"Hello." Ronny nodded and put both his hands on the table when asked to. He had no idea why he did it without question, but he did think he'd be hurt if he didn't comply. "Good for you. It's very nice when someone can follow instructions, don't you think?"

"I don't have any money." The man told him not to lie, but said he didn't need his money. "Then what's with you sitting here like we're friends? I was only having a meal here."

"You've been with someone that has been playing around in the dark magic." He sniffed the air right in front of him. "Yes, it's all over you. Who have you been playing with, Ronald Webber?"

"It's Ronny, not Ronald. No one calls me that." The man just laughed. "What's this about? You the police? I've not done anything wrong, so whatever you got a beef about, I didn't do it."

"Who is he, this man you've been touched by?" He asked him who he was talking about. But instead of answering him, he changed the subject. "I have a gift for you. A lovely one or a bad one, it will depend entirely on what you decide to do."

"I feel like I've been put in one of those whirly things at the fair. Talking to people in this town can give you a headache." Milly came and sat his food in front of him. Ronny just stared at it before looking at the man. "I ordered dinner. That's all. I

131

asked her what it would be, and she said...how the hell am I supposed to eat all this? Dinner was only eight bucks."

She'd given him four of the biggest pieces of fried chicken he'd ever seen, golden brown and looking as crisp as a twig. Mashed potatoes he'd bet were homemade with real potatoes. There was a side plate too, overflowing with green beans with chunks of ham. Fat thick noodles in a creamy gravy, and sliced tomatoes that even smelled fresh. Milly returned to put a basket of rolls in front of him, a crock of butter, and honey too. He looked up at her when she asked him if he needed anything else.

"No. I think my new friend here can join me. Can you bring him a plate too?" She looked at the man, then back at him with a frown. "Never mind. He can just eat what I don't. Thanks, I think we're all right now."

Milly looked at the man then back at him again before shrugging and moving off. He wanted to call her back, ask her how much more he was being charged for the man. Ronny had a feeling they'd filled his plate like this because there were two of them and he was being charged double.

"She can't see me. No one can but you." Ronny told him he didn't care who saw him or not, but he was hungry. "You go on ahead and eat. I'll tell you what I know."

The chicken was so juicy that he moaned. The potatoes were indeed made with actual potatoes, and not flakes like his mom used. He was buttering up his first biscuit—there were six in the basket—when he looked at the gift. It bothered him for some reason that it was sitting there.

"Is that for me?" The man said that it was. "I sure could use me some more cash if that's what is in there. Otherwise, I don't want whatever it is." The man nodded, but said nothing. "You said you were going to tell me what you knew. What is it?"

"The man that is going to get you killed wants you to head west and retrieve a piece of the McCade fortune." Ronny said nothing, but paused in his eating. "You'll never get it, I'm afraid. It's already with the owner, or will be soon enough. I would imagine that any day now she'll be coming here and handing it over to the McCade men, and live happily ever after."

"How do you know she got it? For all you know, it's still sitting there just waiting for me to get." Milly refilled his tea glass and asked him if he was all right. "Yes. Just fine and dandy, thank you. Would you bring my friend here whatever he wants?"

Milly just stared at him, then smiled. "You want me to bring your little friend a dinner too? I'll have to charge you for it, even if he doesn't eat any of it. You sure are nice to your...friends."

"I'm afraid she thinks you quite mad. I've explained to you that no one can see me. You're only making a fool of yourself by talking to others about me. Just tell her that you've changed your mind, that you have no friend." After Ronny repeated what he'd been told to say, Milly walked away. Ronny asked the man what was going on. "I told you, I've come to tell you what I know and to keep you from getting killed over this. Not that I think you'll heed my warning. But I should like to tell you to move on from this. You will only be killed in the end."

"I see. Not really, but let me recap things so we're both on the same page. You're a person that nobody can see, and you've brought me a gift. You also think, and I have no idea why, but you think I should just not do as I was asked, such as go and get a piece of jewelry, on your say so." Ronny snorted, as his mom had done to him a million times. "I don't know, buddy, but I think you're the one that is quite mad. Tell me again how I'm not going to get to the jewelry before the woman does."

"She will have it sooner than you can go out there. If you make it that far. The dragon, he's been talking to her, but she is being most difficult. I think she's having a hard time of it." Ronny said they all were. "Yes, but I believe she feels she is all alone, and will be forever. She won't be once she gets here, but she doesn't know anything about the McCades."

"You mean these men, this family that are supposed to be dragons?" The man grinned and nodded. "And you expect me to just believe this. That there are not only dragons around, but that I should just do as you say."

"If you wish to live, yes. But I have a feeling that you're not going to do any of these things, are you?" Ronny pushed his now empty plate away and pulled the last biscuit out of the basket. "I'm glad you are having a nice meal, Ronald, but I must ask you, is it a good final meal? It will be, should you not listen."

"Who are you?" He said that he couldn't tell him that. "But you think to give me this thing and to warn me off from the man who has said I'd be rich."

"When put that way, yes, I can see where you'd think he was going to follow through. But let me tell you something." Then he simply morphed. The little man sitting there was gone, and in his place was a monster. "I don't think you want to mess with me."

He swiped at Ronny's face, and the claws of the man sitting across from him—a fucking dragon—just barely missed his face. When he opened his mouth, Ronny felt his bladder let go, hot liquid spreading not only down his pant leg but his ass too. Then as suddenly as the dragon was there, he was gone.

Several hours later—he had no idea how he'd gotten

there—Ronny found himself in a large building. Cobwebs hung from the ceiling. Dirt was all over the floor. His pants were soaked, his shoes were missing, and he had the package in his hands. Laughing, spurts of it spilling from his mouth, he opened it.

The gun spilled out of the box. It was a nice one. He flipped it over in his hands several times, looking for anything that might be wrong with it. Some sort of clue as to where it came from. The serial number was gone. Not like it had been filed off, like he'd seen done to some he'd bought, but simply gone. The note, written on thick expensive paper, was tucked in the ribbon on the top of the box.

"To end the deed."

Ronny wasn't sure what that meant. End what deed? Standing up, he tried to mull over the meaning behind the note, and decided that he didn't really care. He had a job to finish.

Almost as soon as he exited the building, he knew what he wanted to do. To hell with the man with the cash, and the other one with the gift. Ronny decided to get himself a piece of the jewelry. And he knew just where a few of them were. Yes, sir. Ronny was going to hold a piece of what was going to make him rich. And thanks to his new friend, he had a gun to do it with.

CHAPTER 10

Dalton made his way to their bedroom. He was really tired, but feeling really good about what he was doing now. And the other cops, men and woman he had worked with, were coming around now to talk, not just to beg him to come back to work. Dalton wasn't going to return to being a cop, and especially not to be in charge of a lot of them. He was happy, relaxed, and loving what he was doing now.

He opened the bedroom door and stopped moving. He wasn't even sure he was breathing as he took in the sight before him.

"I got off work early and thought that I'd surprise you." He was sure that he nodded, because he got to look at Gabriela from head to toe then back again. "I heard you pull in the driveway."

"I drove home." She nodded this time. "I was at work and drove home. You look delicious."

He was making a fool of himself, he knew it. But before him was a vision. A very beautiful, naked one. Going into the room deeper, he tossed his jacket towards the chair. When he heard it hit the floor, he knew that he'd missed. Dalton made his way to the bed where Gabriela was laying and stood over her. When she sat up and reached for him, he held onto the bedpost closest to him. It was that or fall on his ass.

137

"We've been so busy lately that I thought that I'd come here and make things special for you." He told her any more special and he'd be dead. "You say the most romantic things. But I've thought about it a lot, and I want to take your cock into my mouth until you come."

"Christ, love." She grinned at him. "I think there is a streak of something not so nice in you. But I love it, and you. I am at your command."

"Really?" He nodded. "Oh, this might be more fun than I thought. What if I asked you to stand perfectly still so that I can strip you down to your skin? Would you do that?"

Instead of answering her, he put out his arms and stepped back from her. She stood up, her glorious body making his mouth water. Then she was behind him, her arms wrapped around his waist as she started to unbutton his shirt.

Dalton thought of himself as a strong man, one who had on occasion had to look at things that were better left unseen. Nothing horrible, but things that made him wonder at some choices that people made. But right now, with Gabriela taking his clothing off, he was as weak as a kitten. And his decision in letting her do this to him, profoundly scary. She was going to kill him, he thought with a laugh. And really, he didn't care.

When his shirt was pulled off him, his chest bare, Dalton felt her breath on his body, her fingers touching him gently. As she moved around him, her breasts would brush against his skin. Her scent would make his nostrils flare. He was in hell, he knew it.

Her fingers danced over his belt buckle. Closing his eyes made all the sounds in the room, all the things she was doing to him, more pronounced, her touch sexier. The way her warm scent washed over him was wonderful. The snap of his pants sounded loud in the room. Even the opening of his zipper was harsh to his ears. Then she touched him.

His cock burned from the way her hands felt on him. Dalton knew that he was leaking precum, but at this point he thought it was a miracle that he'd not come all over her. And when she pulled his pants down to his thighs, taking his boxers with them, he held his breath as her hair moved over him like a silky curtain.

Dalton put his hands at his side, his fists in tight balls, as she sat on her knees at his cock. He wanted to beg her to take him, to put her silken mouth over his cock, but he was afraid that he'd only make incoherent noises rather than anything that sounded intelligible.

No words were spoken between them as she laid her head on his cock. He did moan; it was about all he could manage at the moment, since he was sure that he had no blood anywhere in his body but his cock. And then she turned to look up at him, her eyes full of need reflecting back. As he watched her, Dalton knew that he loved her, but it hit him hard just how much he did.

This was the woman he was going to spend the rest of his life with. The person who would bear him children, love them as he would. She'd be there for him, forever, and he couldn't think of anyone, not of all the people he'd met in his life, who he'd rather spend it with. Family and his love, it was really all he ever wanted.

Her tongue moved over her lips as he watched, her hands cupped her breasts. When she tugged at her nipples, making them darken with blood, he thought of tasting her there, feeling her breasts fill his mouth. When she looked at him, stared at him as she slowly ran her hand down her body to her navel, Dalton was sure of it now; he was most assuredly in hell.

"If I come like this, will you?" He nodded. "I want to

drink your cum down. Feel you fill my throat with it."

"You're killing me." He sounded strangled, his throat closed off. Gasping for air, he nearly cried out when she licked his length, her tongue wrapped around his crown. "Gabe, please, baby? I'm not going to last, I don't want to. Let me come. Give it to me."

"Not yet."

He reached for something to hold onto when she took him in her mouth. It was hot, wet, and oh so smooth. Her hand held him, her fingers touched places on him that no one had ever touched before. All the while, the entire time she was sucking his cock, her free hand was buried deep within her pussy.

He was so close his balls were full and painful, his heart racing in his chest. Holding onto the post, he fucked her mouth, rolled his hips back and forth as she pleasured them both. And when she threw back her head, commanding him to come, he held his cock, fisting it as his release sprayed her face, arms, and breasts.

Dalton came hard, his body bowing with it, his back aching with a pleasant pain. As he held his cock, tremors like hard punches to his body racking him, he watched her clean herself up with her tongue.

Her lips cleaned his cum from her mouth. Her hands spread his release over her breasts, belly, and ribs. He felt himself grow hard again, his balls fill once more. And when she stood up, moving to the chair not three feet away, he followed her like she was leading him with a leash.

"Fuck me." He nodded as she bent at the waist, her pretty ass right in front of him. Cupping the muscled orbs, he leaned down, kissing each dimple at her cheeks before he moved between her thighs. "I need to come, Dalton. Please fuck me hard."

He slammed forward. He wasn't sure if it was because she had begged him so prettily or his need was taking over, but as he stood there, pounding her pussy as hard as his body could, he leaned over her and slid his finger into her heat. She screamed out a release, and her sheath tightened around him so tightly, he wasn't sure he was able to move. And when he could, he fucked her harder, giving her as much of himself as he could.

Dalton felt his cock moving in and out of her, her pussy wrapped around him so beautifully. Touching her clit, he felt her tighten around him again and again. Knowing that he was close again, his body ready to empty into her, he pinched her clit hard. He felt her not just tighten around him, but strangle his cock. Her sheath milked him to a powerful climax as she screamed out her own climax, over and over again.

His release was powerful. Not only did he feel like he was coming from every part of his body, but pieces of him were being emptied into her as well. His head felt light, his heart pounded. Even his toes felt as if they curled up in his boots until he was weak with it all.

He stood there, leaning over her while he tried to breathe normally. There wasn't any way he could move. He wasn't even sure that he was breathing well enough to get oxygen to his extremities. And when he felt her shift on her feet beneath him, Dalton stood, his knees shaky, and held her to him.

As they both staggered to the bed, all he could think about was what she'd done to him. How she'd made him feel. Dalton thought perhaps if he died right this moment, if he could, he'd be the happiest corpse ever.

"That was amazing." He pulled her to him, kissed her on the forehead and held her as she continued. "I've never done anything like that before. Nothing like that has ever even entered my mind. I think you bring out the depravity in me.

141

I'm not saying I don't like this new me, but it's so unexpected too."

"Anytime you have a thought like that enter your head, you just go with it. However, not too many times in one day. I could have a massive stroke. Christ, seeing you there, naked? It was the best thing I think I've ever walked in on in my life." He laughed with her. "I sound like a teenager who's just gotten laid for the first time in his life. Actually, that's how I feel right now. Like you are my first. And you'll forever be my last. I love you."

He held her, stroking her back as they lay there. Dalton knew that she slept after a little while. He too dozed in and out. And when his phone rang from across the room, he didn't even bother getting up. If it was family or an emergency, they knew how to contact him. After a few more minutes, he went to sleep.

~~~

Gabe was in the kitchen when a truck pulled into the drive. Dalton had left her about an hour ago, saying that he had to go in and learn how to order for the diner. She said she'd be just fine, but now she wasn't sure what to do. There were no deliveries coming that she knew of, so she stayed in the house as the man got out and looked around the yard.

It occurred to her for some reason that he wasn't there on a social visit. The way he walked around and not to the house was sort of…it was kind of distracting. The pickup truck he was in was brand new, the plates the paper, temporary kind of plates. She was just going to call out to someone, anyone in the family, to ask if they knew what was going on when she felt something behind her.

The hand over her mouth had her screaming ineffectually. Gabe could smell the person. Drugs. Old wine. Body odor. Then she felt the pinch of something in her arm and knew that she'd been drugged. As she fell into the abyss, she tried her best to reach out to Dalton to help her. She thought of Jasmine, as they had a date later today for shopping before they left in the morning.

Blue truck with alloyed wheels. Man with green shirt, dark hair in it. Man has me drugged. Jasmine asked her where she was. *Home. I'm fading fast.*

I'm coming. I'm with Jorden. We're coming. She wasn't sure they were going to make it. Her body was too weak to fight them off as the man outside joined the guy who had hit her. *Gabe, can you call the dragons?*

The dragons. She'd forgotten about them. *Come to me, my babies.* Her head hit something hard, her body too. By the time she realized that she was in the back of the truck, it was moving. Closing her eyes, Gabe let the drugs take her over.

When she woke she was in a dark room, so dark that she couldn't make out even the smallest of details. There was a sliver of light under what she assumed was a doorway, but nothing more. It wasn't until she sat up that she realized both her feet and hands had been restrained.

Do not move overly much. She knew the voice but shied away from it. The dragon, Roderick, was with her. *We were too late to keep you from being taken, but we are here now, to protect you. Should we have killed the men, as was our plan, you would have been hurt badly when the truck was moving.*

"Where are Dalton and the others? They're not hurt, are they?" Roderick told her that all were safe. "Good. I'm glad. I...that man was in our house."

Yes, he used magic to enter. The other man, the younger of the two, he was there to distract you long enough for the elder one to enter. They will both be taken care of today, my lady. She asked him what they wanted, even though she was pretty sure she knew. *They are here for the jewels...yours, as you have guessed.*

They will not get them. The one that drove you here, he thinks that they are things he can simply take from you. Or perhaps for you to hand over. He has much knowledge, but not enough to know that you are the wearer of them and they cannot be removed.

She reached for Dalton and the pain of her head took her breath away. Lyna told her not to try again, that they had informed the family that they were with them. Gabe had not even realized that Lyna was there as well, but was glad for it. Gabe asked what had happened to her.

There are three here. Two of them you have had contact with, the other we have yet to ascertain. The oldest of the three, older by a great many years, is the one with the most magic. He has put a spell on you so that you cannot contact the family without causing great pain to your head, as you have figured out. Gabe lay down as Lyna continued. *We have been advised to hold off killing any of them until we have more information. Information, we've been told, that will help someone find out who has been financing this horrific mess.*

"They think there is just one person that is doing this to us? How is that possible? I thought they killed off each man as they came to them." Neither of them said anything. "Unless he's having them do his dirty work while he sits back and reaps the profits."

I believe that is what your family thinks as well. Also, I am to tell you something from Lady Aisha. She said to tell you that if you let them hurt you, she will be sorely disappointed in you. Gabe laughed. *I find it most strange that she thinks you have any say over them hurting you.*

"I think she's kidding." Roderick said he hoped so. "Now, do we have a plan? Am I just to wait for them to try to hurt me? I'd really like something to focus on. And could you please tell Dalton that I love him very much?"

Roderick moved…she heard him shuffle across the floor.

Then there was a small flare of light and she could see them both. The light, like the dragons, was blue, and she moved a little closer to it for warmth. She wasn't sure if she was cold or just terrified, and needed the normalcy of this. Either way, she felt better for it.

Lord Dalton said to tell you that he loves you so very much as well. She felt her eyes fill with tears. *He also said to tell you that he is coming for you and for you to sit tightly. I'm sorry, tight. He said for you to sit tight.*

"Thank you for that, Roderick. I'm going to sit here like a good girl and wait. But what do we know of these men?" Roderick said they knew little to nothing as yet, but would soon enough. "Are you going to be all right? I mean, I don't want you hurt either in this."

I will be fine, my lady, this I promise you. She nodded and asked about the bindings at her arms and legs. *You can remove them better than we would be able to. We could cut them, but with our claws, it might harm you unnecessarily. Just think of something sharp and use that.*

She felt the handle of the scalpel in her hands before the thought was complete. Turning it carefully in her hands — she knew that it would be sharp — she cut through the tape as she thought of the man outside of her house.

"You said he was a distraction. How did you figure that out? And why didn't he come to the door? I mean, I saw him in the yard, and I'm assuming that he was supposed to be a distraction, but he looked…I was going to say stupid, but that's not right. He was drugged, I think." Roderick told her that he didn't smell of drugs. "Then I don't know. Maybe I'm just thinking on this too hard."

In looking into his mind, I think him to have a higher opinion of himself than is right. He thinks himself to be brilliant, but he is only average. Slightly lower than average of the normal human, really. The first layer of tape was finished, and she cut into the second one as Lyna spoke again. *He has taken you in the hopes of getting one of the pieces of jewelry to hold until all the others are together. A bargaining chip, he calls it. I don't think he would have ever been able to make that work. There are other forces that he would have had to contend with.*

"What do you mean?" She cut her hand then, not paying attention, she knew. "You don't think we can make this work? That we'll fail in getting the pieces all together?"

No, I don't believe that at all. I only think that the other out there, he will be difficult to work around until he's killed. He, this other man, he holds a great deal of power. I think that is why when we arrived at the house, we could not see anything amiss. It wasn't until the truck that had you in the rear of it moved from the perimeter that we could see it. At first we thought that we had missed it. But it could have been shielded from us. The tape was off her hands, but she had to massage them several times before she could pick up the scalpel again. Lyna continued. *There is very dark magic going on with this group, Roderick. Do you think that —?*

Do not say it. Do not. We don't have enough information to know anything for a certainty, and without the spark that gives us full power, we aren't going to know. Gabe looked at the two of them when Roderick cut his mate off. *We need to stay positive; all will fail if we do not.*

"Spark? And before we get too far off the path here, how did that scalpel appear in my hands just when I needed it?" The noise outside the door had her slicing through the tape at her legs quickly. Gabe knew that she couldn't move, not without a little more blood running to her feet, but she was going to make them pay for taking her. When the door opened she lashed out.

"Gabe? Don't hurt me." Vance? He was here too? His whispered words were both comforting and scary at the same time. "I'm going to lean down to you so we can talk. Just don't hurt me, all right?"

"How did you get in here?" He just laughed a little. "Okay, I guess I don't want to know. But are we going to leave now? I'd really like to get out of here."

"I have to take care of a couple of things first. But I didn't want you running out of here and getting in the way. Do you think you can wait for a few more minutes? I promise to come back for you if you would." She told him about the dragons. "Good. I wondered if you'd been able to call them to you. I'm glad that you have protection. But if it's okay with you, I'll take Roderick with me. I could use a good…dragon to help with clean up, if it comes to that."

"All right, but neither of you are to be hurt, do you hear me?" He nodded, then kissed her on the forehead. "Vance, I don't mean to sound ungrateful or anything, but could you just get this done so I can go home?"

"My pleasure." She felt rather than saw him stand up. He was a big man…she thought him bigger even more so than Dalton. But when he leaned down to her, she held herself steady as he whispered in her ear. "They're right outside the door. You have to trust me when I tell you to turn around and not look. All right?"

Nodding, she turned around. She was sure that whatever happened next she wasn't going to like. So when the door opened, the bright light letting her know, she heard a gun fire, screaming, then nothing.

The hand that touched her was firm and she nearly screamed. The small whimper that fell from her lips was met with a laugh, and she knew it was Vance. The man had saved her. Turning around as she was helped up, she held him to her and cried. Relief so profound made her sobby and emotional.

Vance held her, and when she was calmer, he asked if she

wanted to go. Nodding, he helped her out of the building, and soon she was standing in the daylight. He held her hand, letting her sob out how happy she was that he'd come for her, before he lifted her chin up and looked down at her face.

"I have to go." She told him to stay and talk to his family. "I can't. I've been talking to them and they understand, but I can't be found here. Not yet."

She looked around and realized she was in what the rest of them were calling the warehouse district. It was also where the cigarettes were being held. He nodded when she turned back to look at him.

"You're undercover. And can't be seen talking to the police. I'm sorry, Vance. I hope this didn't mess it up." He said that she hadn't, that he had been nearby when she needed him. "I don't understand, but I know that you're working. Go before the police get here."

"I'm sorry, love. I truly am. And before you ask, Roderick and his mate are going to clean up inside for me. There won't be any prints from me being here." She nodded. "I hate to tell you this, but there were only two men inside. The third one, the one that Roderick spoke of with the magic, he isn't here. I don't know where he went, but he's gotten away."

"Will he come back before Dalton gets here?" He shook his head. "You're sure? You know he won't come back and finish me off?"

"Lyna is watching you. Roderick told me that he had to go back to his host. I'm assuming he meant Grady. But Lyna said she was staying. It was her duty to keep you safe." She looked just inside the building that they'd come out of. "No one will come after you, Gabe. On this, I can bet my life."

"Don't. Don't say that. I don't want anyone betting their life for mine. I get it, I'll be safe. But you have to be too." He nodded. "No. You have to say it, Vance. I don't know you well…I'd like to, but I do know that you're a haunted man, and that you do more for this family than the rest of them combined. But if you tell me, straight out, that you'll be safe, then I know you will. You won't break your promise to me."

"No, I would never do that. Not to any of you. But I will tell you this, it's the best I can do…I will be as safe as I can make myself. Is that all right?"

She nodded.

He kissed her on the forehead and then left her there. She watched the area, knowing that as soon as someone came she'd be fine. Looking over at Lyna, she asked her to come closer to her.

You are unwell? She told the little dragon that she just needed comfort. *I can help you with that.*

As the dragon moved closer, Gabe could feel her heat. It was strangely comforting, like being wrapped in a thick warm blanket. Or comforting arms.

"I guess there are others coming to see us. I wonder if they'll be like you in size or bigger."

Some will be quite large. But as you can guess, they have powers that keep them well hidden. There will even be some that are smaller than me. She sat close enough to her that Gabe could touch her. She reached out and ran her fingers over the scales that covered her chest. They weren't hard like she thought they would be, but more slick. *I knew of one once, he was as large as some of your buildings on your land. He was cumbersome, to say the least, but he was as friendly as he was fierce when he was in battle mode. I have forgotten his name; he was a good dragon, but not a good warrior. I think he was killed from wounds that he sustained from war.*

"I guess there were plenty of wars in your lifetime. I've heard of a few of them that were as bloody as any had ever been. Did you know Warrior?" She said that they all knew him and the queen. "I guess you've been around for a very long time."

Yes, very long. We have been waiting, my mate and I, for the right McCade family to come along. We've never been released before, not since we were put upon the back of Williamston, son of Caelin, as a sigil. Gabe asked about the first Caelin. *He was a good man, better father than most in his time. He would take the time to play with his sons, all six of them, every day. And when it came time for them to learn their letters, to read and cipher, he was there with them, teaching them the way of numbers too. But he wasn't a man to cross either. I saw him once beat a man to death for harming his cattle. It was horrific, but fair. The foods that we had, they were limited to what we could keep. This man only wanted to harm his family by killing off his only source of trade, or milk.*

"I heard that he killed his father. Removed his head from his shoulders to avenge his mother's demise." Lyna cocked her head at her. "Caelin said to his mother, I think I heard, that he'd kill his father for what he did to their family and home. He did kill him, didn't he?"

Lord Butler is not dead, my lady. Neither is the son, Caelin. I'm not sure where you might have heard such a thing. Lord Caelin is an immortal. His father…he has used black magic to live so long, but as I have said, they are both living. Gabe stood up, her head buzzing with the information. Lord Butler was alive, and so was his son? *I know that the son, he has been around the area for some time. I think you have seen him as well.*

Gabe started shaking her head. There was too much… not just information, but everything that their being alive indicated. The man had told her that he worked for someone. Waterson. His name had been….

"No. Not the little man with the present." Lyna said that was him. "No, he said his name was Peterson. That he worked for a man named Waterson. That the man left me the package when he passed away."

Lyna laughed. *Peterson is the name of Lord Caelin's page. Waterson? Let me think.... Ah yes, Lord Waterson is the man who was his financial advisor. He also cared for young Caelin when he was just a small boy. Kept him from his father's sight, I believe. He also helped him improve his sword work, and how to — are you unwell?*

"They're alive. They're both alive and out there. This can't be right, Lyna. Do you have any idea what this means to us? Not just me, but the family. If they're out there, what does that mean for the jewels? Should we...? Are we going to...? Lyna, this is too much." Lyna nodded. "Do they know about each other?"

You mean that the other is living? Yes, I believe they have knowledge that the other is alive. What are you thinking, Lady Gabriela?

She had so many thoughts going through her head right now it was hard to capture just one and tell her. But one thing she knew for sure, they were against a great many more odds than before.

"I think that I know who is financing the men to come and kill us. To take the jewels that he thought he should have." Lyna asked her if she meant Lord Butler. "Yes. And Caelin, his son, I think he's working to stop him. Holy fuck balls, we're so screwed right now."

151

CHAPTER 11

Butler moved with ease through the throng of people. He didn't care for them as a general rule, but sometimes, like now, he needed them. Today of all days, he needed to have some of the anger, the energy that he craved. Sitting at one of the benches in front of the food court, he waited. It wouldn't be long before some kid and his mother would come here to give him what he needed.

Children were the strongest life force he could use. Their anger was white hot for only the briefest of times, but it was full of energy too. In less than two minutes there was a woman with three little kids, and each of them had the look of overprivileged little shits that just did not give two fucks what their mother wanted. This would be good.

The first fight began over the seating arrangements. It was fifteen minutes of threats that would never be acted upon, crying, and a temper tantrum. He got the most magic from the tantrum, but he enjoyed it all.

After an hour, still no food gathered but a great deal of magic for him, Butler moved on. There was more to be found in the mall, and he was going to enjoy every single bit of it. Walking past one of the larger department stores, he paused in front of a show window. He saw a woman there that reminded him of Prisane.

The queen, the bitch. She'd been nothing like he thought she should have been. He wanted a woman to warm his bed, to bear him sons, and to turn a blind eye to what he did to entertain himself. She had done none of those things. In fact, Butler was very sure that she went out of her way to be so opposite of what he wanted that he wished that he'd had the opportunity to kill the fucking bitch.

Well, she had born him a son, one that he'd known nothing about until later when he'd come to see him. By then Butler had been broke, looking for his next bride to sire him a brood of sons. And he'd been dabbling in the magic that had sustained him all these years.

But the women had been failures. None of them, not a single mistress, wife, or even raped female, had given him anything but more useless females. It was as if he'd been cursed. And if he was, he knew just who to blame for that as well. That fucking Prisane.

His son was so much like his mother that Butler hated him on sight. The kid, a man really, had come to him to kill him. He might have, too, if Butler hadn't had a little more magic up his sleeve than the kid had. He'd been surprised by that, and for that one time he'd had the upper hand in things. But not so much since.

"You think to kill me, your own father? For what reason? I've done nothing to you. You should be happy that you even breathe because of me." He laughed and told him that it was his destiny. "Destiny? Your only destiny, son, is to come to me when I call you and to help me find your mother and that fortune. I'd even be willing to share it with you if you'd help."

"You're never going to find it, and I am not a son of yours." Butler had laughed at the stupidity of the statement. How did he think he'd gotten here without his seed? "Mother sent me to find you…she prepared me for this day. I'm going to end your life, as someone should have decades ago."

The sword that he pulled from his scabbard was beautiful. Butler would bet anything that it was a part of the McCade holdings. Holdings that he'd never been able to find in three decades of looking. He pulled his own sword, cheap and not of much use against the one that would cut into him. And cut him he had, too, over and over with the thing. Even now, after all this time, the pain of those very cuts would ache him, even bleed at times. And reasoning with him hadn't helped at all.

"We should come together, you and I. See what we have missed over the years. I think I should like to see what you have—"

The sword sliced through the air, not an inch from his face. Had he leaned in to give his son his hand, he would have been beheaded. He was sure that had been his plan. Butler didn't even know his name, much less his age or anything about him. And he thought he wasn't going to get the chance, either. Not at the rate the encounter was going.

"Stop this. I am your father, and I demand that you stop this nonsense this moment." The younger version of his mother stood there, the tip of his blade resting in the ground between his feet. The grin on his face was so much like his mother's that it was as if he was staring right at her. He was neither winded nor sweaty, the opposite of himself. "You cannot wish to kill me. I have much to offer you. A fortune of jewels and other sundry. Come, let us raise a tankard in honor of your dearly departed mother."

"My mother was a saint, and I doubt overly much that you wish to raise anything to her but your fist should she be here. I know what you did to her. Nay, I will not drink with you in her honor, when you did nothing but harm and tear everything apart that she worked so hard for her entire life."

Butler laughed. It was funny even now to think that she

had worked. Women were of no use when it came to working, but for housework and bearing sons. Butler was a man, a great man, and all females, as far as he was concerned, were of no use other than to spread their legs and give him a son. His son, he'd not understood that. He doubted much that he did even now.

"What is it you think I did to her? Hit her? Yes, it was my duty to keep her in line when she wished to run over me. Did I spend the money, my money when I wed her, on things that she did not care for? Again, I did that. But what right did she have to tell me what I could do with the money I earned by marrying the wretch?" He watched the boy, and wondered where he'd been hidden. Who had been there when she'd birthed him? "Is it because I took others to my bed? It was my duty to sire a son, one that I knew about. She deserved whatever came to her by lying to me about my son. She did this to herself, the lying cunt."

"And why do you think she lied to you? Because she felt you'd teach me your ways of life?" Butler said yes, it was what he would have done. "I am happier than you can know that she kept me from you. She herself trained me in the art of sword play. How to wield a blade, fight a man with my fist. Mother showed me the way to treat a person, be it woman or man. She taught me more in the years I was with her than you could have ever imparted to me. Mother might have lied to you, but she had her reasons. And before me stands the main reason you were never told about me. You're a monster."

Butler had decided to ignore the comment about him being a monster. Even then, he'd thought of himself as more than that. Now? He supposed he was that and more. And Butler loved it. He snorted at the things his wife had taught his son, knowing that he'd be better at everything if he'd done it.

"Sissy things. Woman's ways. Did she also teach you to wash laundry? Perhaps she showed you how to cook your lazy wife a dinner? I'm sure that any woman you take to your home will be happy to know that a mere woman taught you how to be a man." The kid laughed then, threw back his head with it. "You think this funny? That you're a failure of a man?"

"Am I, Father? How many other sons have you sired? I have six sons, all of them young men that I can be proud of. And they will have sons, six each as well, until a time comes when the McCades will be whole again." Butler called him a liar. "Nay, I am not. I know that you have had nothing but female children. Twenty-three girls, not a son among them, is there? And would you like to know why? I know. Mother cursed you. Or some would think that she saved the world from the sons that you might have had."

"She cannot do that to me." Again the laughter, so much like his mother's that he wanted to run him through. He told him that she had and still did it even now. "You will tell me where she is, and I will deal with her this moment."

"Mother is far beyond your reach, Father. But she sent me in her stead. I will give you the punishment that you so richly deserve." Butler asked him what he thought he'd done wrong. "Breathed."

The sword arced through the air, slicing his arm from shoulder to wrist, rendering his arm useless. As the blade swung back and forth, cutting more and more into his flesh but never giving the killing blow, Butler tried in vain to kill his son. Not only was his son's blade far superior, but his skill as a swordsman was excellent. Then he took Butler to the ground.

"You will stand there and end my life? The man that gave you what you have?" The boy asked him what he thought he'd given him. "Life. Without me, you would have not have existed."

"You are wrong about that." The blade moved slowly into his belly, his body too beaten and drained of energy to fight any longer. "I shall see you again, Father. And when I do, I shall sit back while your grandson, many generations from now, slices your head from your shoulders."

Since that day and many days and years after, he would look at the wound in his belly—not a scar as it should have been, but a long slice of a cut, the width of the blade that had put it there—and think of those words. His grandson, a son of his son's children, might come and ruin his life.

It was why he'd killed them, the preceding McCades, that had been born. It mattered little to him if it was a female or a male, so long as the circle of them, the power of the name, could not harm him. Until this generation. This one, they'd been the hardest of all of them to even get close to. And he had tried, every day for decades. Even with the piece that he'd harbored for all these years in his possession, he was still afraid.

Butler realized that he'd been standing in front of the store for too long and moved on. There were times, like today, when his magic was simply too weak to keep his appearance as he liked. Young and vibrant. A face and body that women would fawn over. The children's anger had only served to make some of his aches and pains go away. And there were plenty of those too.

Had he had the money and jewels, as were his to do with as he pleased, then he could find him another witch. Have her give him enough magic so that he no longer had to suck energy from those around him. Twice now over the decades he'd found such a person to give him the magic to keep him alive, and both times they'd only given him as much as his coin could pay for. Butler was not able to promise them money that he did not have long ago. Only now, in this time, was he able to procure money to spend and use. They seemed to know much more about him than he thought good. It was then that he hit upon the idea to advertise about the jewels and the legend. And to have others find them for him.

It had been his plan to put out as little information as he could about the set. The fact that one of them had been broken down into two pieces wasn't common knowledge, but he soon found out that a lot of details, more than he'd had, were there for the taking. He wondered briefly if it had been his son who had done that, made it difficult for him to get anyone to do the job for him.

His fourth wife, the fourth woman that he had taken to his bed after Prisane, had said the necklace was too heavy for her delicate neck, that it hurt her to wear it. And in his happiness to have a son, which she promised him the child she was fat with would be, he did just as she wished. It had been one of the biggest mistakes of his life.

Butler had lost both pieces soon after that. It had been the witch's payment, when she said she would help him with the magic. He had no idea how she'd found out about the jewels, nor at that time had he cared. He would have had a long life.

It had been his plan to kill her when she had done the deed, then take back the pieces. But she had been long gone before he had recovered enough to chase her down for them. Now all he had was one part of the beautiful and cursed necklace.

He thought about the only piece that he'd been able to find in all his years of killing off the McCades. The family had had others. He was sure of it. But all he'd been able to gather was that one. Butler couldn't understand why that was, but with this generation, he was afraid that even that might not be enough to get to what was rightfully his.

Butler knew there were dragons. He'd seen them his entire life when he'd been a kid, then through his married life with Prisane. She would ride that monster of hers until he nearly wanted to kill her to make her come back and behave. But he never hurt her when the monster was around. He'd learned that the hard way.

The dragon had made him pay for the one time Butler had lost his temper with Prisane. The dragon had been there in the same room. The large beast of a warrior had come up off the floor and attacked. His wings had knocked him to the wall, his hot breath had burned his skin. He thought the only reason that he'd not killed him was that he wore his crown. Butler never took it off again, even to go to the privy, for fear that was the only thing that would save him again.

Now here he was, within touching distance of four of the other pieces, and he couldn't get them. Not even close enough to see which useless female held which item. He needed more, any of them, but all he had was the necklace and nothing else. He knew he was never going to see the monies until he had them all.

There had been riches too, he'd seen them. Chests of gems and stones. There had been bolts of cloth. Spices from faraway lands. Paintings from great artists. He knew that most of that, the material and foodstuff, would be rotted by now, but the chests would be…should have been his. He was the man of the castle, and she had deprived him even of that.

Great portraits of bygone McCades were there, even one of him and his wife, the traitorous bitch. There had been pottery and carpets. Of course he'd stolen most of it, right from under her nose, when he'd been there. Sold it off when she told him he was to have no more. But there had been things, a great many pieces of furniture, the throne he so loved sitting upon, and even the books that lined many of the shelves in the library. Books that he'd never touched them because he'd not learned to read.

She rubbed that in his face as well, offering to teach him his letters and numbers. But that had been of no use to him then, and less so even now. Butler was king then, and he thought of himself as such now. Kings did not worry over what was written in books, of all things.

Making his way to his little hovel, he put away the items that he'd taken for himself. New shirts and a jacket. A pair of leather boots and a coat. He never thought of it as stealing. That would mean that it wasn't his for the taking, and everyone knew that kings took what they wanted. There would be plenty enough people bowing before him soon enough, he knew, and he wanted to look his best when that time came.

Sitting on the only piece of furniture that he'd been able to bring here, he looked around the place. It was only temporary, he told himself, and his chair, a cheap version of the one he'd sat upon so long ago, would be replaced. Soon, very soon now, he'd have his castle back, and servants. And then he'd deal with his son.

"Caelin, you are going to be very sorry you were ever born." Laughing, he leaned back in his seat. Plotting and planning had never been his strong suit, but he thought that he'd done well thus far. Hire others to find the pieces, pay them with a bullet or poison, or even use another person working for him, and he'd never have to pay out.

Frowning, he thought of his plan so far as somewhat of a failure. No one, not a single one of the men he'd had working for him, had been able to produce a single piece. He was going to have to get better men. Not like the fools he'd had before, but men who would not hesitate to kill to get the pieces. Ronny—what a sissy name—had gotten him the female as he'd said, but he must have been followed or something. The man who'd killed him and the other man had shown no mercy when dealing with either of the two men.

Butler knew that he'd only gotten out with moments to spare. Whatever had come for them, whatever man had been there to save the woman, had been good. In and out, not a sound had been made. The only thing that had saved Butler's life had been the fact that he'd had to piss. Upon returning to go and get her piece, Butler had found the room torched, the men dead, and the woman gone too. Butler knew that he'd been gone only a few moments. Yes, Butler thought, he only survived it because he'd had a full bladder.

"I'll have to make them heel to me. These men and women, these people will know my wrath before this is all done." Lying down on the blow up mattress he'd been able to take, Butler felt confident in his proclamation. They would know their place or he'd show it to them. And perhaps he'd have a bit of the woman too. While her mate watched. No, he'd not do that. Shivering once, he rolled to his side and closed his eyes. Soon, he told himself. Soon.

~~~

"Does anyone know where he might be?" Dalton wanted to tell Kenton that if they knew where this man was, wouldn't they have sent someone to take care of him by now? But he didn't. His temper was short enough without having his brother pissed off at him too. He looked over at Gabe.

She'd been so quiet since he'd picked her up from the warehouse not two hours ago. After telling them what she'd heard from Lyna and having it confirmed by Roderick, she'd fallen silent. Dalton had asked her several times if she was all right, but her answer had been the same…she was fine, just thinking.

Sitting down beside her, he took her hand in his and held it. Whatever she was thinking, he'd not been able to breach

162

her mind to figure it out. It was too…well, it was just too everything.

Her mind was bouncing between medical jargon and the conversation with Lyna. Then she'd be on a shopping trip, back to the emergency room, and then.... He looked at her when she touched on the memory of the boy and the dragon. Then her mind calmed and he spoke to her.

"Who was he?" She shrugged and shook her head. "The child was dead, yet he spoke to you. How was that possible?"

"I don't know. He gave me this." She pulled the little chain out of her blouse and showed him the dragon on the chain. "He handed it to me. Then a few hours later, this little man, a man that I now know is your long lost...I'm not even sure how many grandfathers back he is, but he comes in and gives me a little box with the hair things in it. I haven't...I'm trying my best to work this out, but I'm lost."

"I am as well." He looked around the room…his family was all there. Gavin and his mom, brothers, and sisters-in-law. They were all working on this problem as if it were their job. He supposed in a way, it really was.

"The little man, I have a feeling that he's not so little or as old as he looked to me. He was...I know this sounds odd, but I think he was projecting an image that made me feel safe with him. Like a little old man that meant no harm." He said that it made perfect sense to him. "So he comes into my office, and tells me this story about dragons. I didn't believe him, of course, but...."

She got up and began pacing. His family did that as well. Jorden, he thought, was the best at it…he mumbled to himself, used his hands a lot, and usually came to a good answer or solution to whatever he was working out. But Gabe just paced quietly, and without using her hands. It was sort of calming.

"I don't think there was even a little boy." He asked her

163

what she meant. "Well, a week or so after the incident—and that's what I'm calling it because anything else makes me ill—but a week later I realized that I had no death certificate to sign. There had been no one coming in and asking me about it. So I looked him up. There was nothing in the paper. Not a single mention on the news, and I couldn't find the family either. I think…that was a cruel thing to do, don't you think? To play on my emotions like that. Using a child."

"Yes, it was. But I'm glad that it was done that way. I mean, that no one was killed. I see little of it here, but when a child is killed, even just dies from some sickness, it takes a great deal out of me." Gabe sat down across from Dalton. "He got your attention, right? He made you remember it, to take the dragon from him."

"I think that's when he marked me. Not like the other women, but silently, like he didn't want me chased when I came here by…. Well, by his father. The dragon, Caelin, he didn't hound me like I heard he did with the others. There was no guiding me here with the promise of riches. Nothing like that at all." He nodded, not exactly liking where this was going, but thinking she was correct. "There was a shield around me, sort of. I was able to not just get here without much in the way of trouble, but we met and came together because I didn't have all this other drama going on with it."

I do not think I hounded anyone, my lady. But I do believe that you may be right. That young Caelin has brought you here. She laughed when Dalton did at the tone of the dragon's voice. *The charm that you wear, I think it is what kept you safe, as you have said. And I'm sure that he will do the same for the other two women. They will have their own piece of magic that will keep them safe for the same reason.*

The others joined them. His mom sat there very quietly, and watched them as they took turns making assumptions about who would be next, how safe she'd be when she traveled, and what she'd have as the next piece.

"I think he has one." They all turned to her. "The father. I think he'd have a piece of the set. I don't know which piece, but he'd have one. That would be his bargaining chip."

"How did you come to that conclusion? And I'm not saying that you're wrong, but tell me how you got there." She smiled at Kenton when he laughed. "Mom, you're scary right now. You know something, what is it?"

"Let's assume for a moment that he has one piece. And for this, we'll say he has...I don't know. He has the necklace. That was the one piece that was left behind, Caelin told us that. As did the queen. So this king, Butler, gave it to his new wife and she wore it. After a time, however, he had it broken down into two pieces for one of them...I can only assume that he had more than just a couple of wives in his lifetime." Dalton nodded. "Okay. We know that he doesn't have the four pieces that we have. The necklace was made into the torques that Harper wears and the necklace. He has to have that piece. He would have kept it, I think, to have when the other pieces where found. Like I said, his bargaining chip to hold over our heads."

"You think he had anything to do with the other generations dying before it was complete?" Mom told Kenton that she didn't think so, it wouldn't have benefited him to do that. "I don't know, Mom. From what I've come to understand about the man, things were to be his way or he'd kill you off. No, I think he's had a heavy hand in making sure that this curse, for whatever reason, didn't come about. But okay, he has one of the pieces. So how does the woman come here? I mean, there is nothing guiding her if she has no jewelry."

"No one guided Gabe either, but here she is. I think — and this is just this old woman speaking — I think that the son

165

will protect them as best he can from his father." All of them, him included, denied their mother being old. "But what do you think of my theory? I mean, he had to start somewhere, correct?"

"So he has this piece. What then? Will he come here, take the pieces from us, and then raise...." Emma stopped speaking and her face paled. "He's a McCade. I mean, not by birth, but he married Prisane and became a McCade, right?"

Caelin asked to have a moment to see how that worked. Dalton was almost afraid of the answer. He knew it was going to be just as Emma said. He'd come here, kill the women and children, then them, and then take the jewelry for himself. Then he'd call forth the dragons and win. Win what, he had no idea, but they'd all be dead and he'd end the legend for all time.

"He did not take her name. And there was no love between them. They were not mates." Dalton asked him what that meant. "It means that he is not a true McCade. Without being born of one nor being loved, truly loved, by a female in this family, there is no connection to the jewelry for him. He will not be able to call me or the other dragons. He will not have the ability to see the magic that calls to him either. The jewels, to him, will be ordinary in color and beauty."

"You mean that he might, for all we know, have one of the many copies. I don't see that happening, do you? I mean, he had the piece from the beginning. He would have known the piece as well as we do. But that's not going to do us a lot of good in the end, will it? We'll still all be dead and he'll have the set." Jasmine said they'd just tell him that he wasn't the right kind of McCade to call them forth. Kenton was shaking his head even before she finished speaking. "No. I mean, we could tell him, no problem. But it's doubtful that he'd believe us. And to get that close to him, to let him know? That would be like giving him the keys to this all, and we know it. He won't believe it until all the pieces are together, we're all dead, and it doesn't work."

"Well that just sucks." Dalton laughed. His mother just didn't speak that way. "If it's all the same to you boys, I'd just as soon you not get killed. Not that I know how that would work with us all being immortal and all, but I'm sure that if we think on it, there is a way." Kenton told them all what the dragon had told them earlier. That he had to do the killing. Caelin spoke before they could continue on their good news.

If he is with us all when I'm called, then he can order me to kill you all. Even though he is not a McCade, he is forever my king until someone else comes along and makes it not so. Dalton wasn't sure what that meant, not really. There was something there, something he wasn't getting, but he was too strung out to think right now. And so was his family, apparently.

After they all left, he sat on the couch with Gabe and held her. He was terrified of losing her and the rest of his family.

CHAPTER 12

Lewis sat in his newly remodeled restaurant. He'd been working on it for so long that he despaired of ever getting it completed. He looked around at the finished tables, the accents on the walls and other areas, even the pretty rugs had been put in places to warm the room up.

There was a section for a coat girl, a checkout place, and a hostess station. The soft drink machine had been set up a week ago, the beverages brought in today and tested. And yet he wasn't sure it was a good idea to open the place. Or even, for that matter, if he could open it after all this work.

Two weeks ago he'd been on cloud nine. None of his family had guessed he'd been in here working after dark, after he'd worked all day with one or all of his brothers on their homes. His mother had known, of course; she was hard to hide anything from. But none of his brothers or sisters-in-law knew. And now he was done. Even the menus, something that he'd slaved over for a month, were printed and stuck in the new menu holders he'd had specially made.

The Dragon's Lair, the name he'd come up with for his new venture on the spur of the moment, was printed on the front. A beautiful blue dragon stared back at him from its place under the name. And now, as he sat there, he wondered what he'd been thinking. His mate was coming, and he was ill prepared for her.

If not the next one arriving, then soon after he'd have his mate. A prospect he wasn't sure he was looking forward to. Not that he wouldn't do his best by her, but he also was terrified of what she'd want from him. Women in general, as far as he was concerned, were simply scary beings.

The others had their mates. Not he or Vance, but they were coming. Lewis did smile at the thought of the woman who would be for his brother. A woman would have to be pretty brave to try and come to terms with Vance. Of course, she might be just what he needed in a wife. Someone to take away the shadows.

My lord. Lewis sat very still, not knowing the voice that had spoken to him. But he had a good idea it was the dragon. He also knew what it meant for him to be able to speak to him. *I was hoping t'would be you. The thought of talking to Lord Vance frightens me just a little.*

"You? You're a dragon. How are you afraid of my brother?" Lewis laughed. "Okay. Never mind. I know the answer to that already. He's a little different than the rest of us."

He is, sir. Very much so. I will assume, since you and I can speak now, that the new miss is coming for you. Lewis nodded, saddened by the thought. *You're not happy? The woman who comes here, she was born just for you. For this time in your life. A mate for all eternity. Someone to —*

"Yes, I get it. And I don't know how I feel, to be honest. I have my life the way I want it. Things are going well for me at this moment. I'm not sure how a mate would fit in." He told him very well, from what he'd seen of the others. "Yes, but I'm not sure how I'm to go about helping her. In the event that you've not noticed this about me, I'm not an artist like Jorden. I don't have a great job that keeps me busy like Grady does.

Kenton has his job saving lives. Dalton is working as a cook in the diner. Me? I have an empty building that I thought could make a great restaurant."

Is there a reason that you've changed your mind about that? From what I hear from the others, you are quite the cook. He told him he was a chef. *Then chef. What is holding you back from doing just what you want?*

"A mate." He wasn't sure that was a good answer, but it was the only one that he had. A mate would change things. She'd want to do things her own way, have certain things in order. It was why other than taking out the furniture that he had no use for, he'd done nothing to his home other than paint the walls a sort of white color and take up the carpets. He was waiting.

You think a woman would want you to be different? For you not to be as happy as you can be? Lewis said he had no idea. *That is very true. But for all you know, she could be someone that is as lost about a relationship as you. Or she could be...I believe that Gavin calls it a ballbuster. His teacher is like that. I have no idea what that means, but I get the feeling that it isn't a compliment.*

Lewis laughed. "No, it's not. And I'd not say that around my mom or his mom. Mine would start keeping a list of things to reprimand you for when you're released. And Jasmine would more than likely want to know where you'd heard that, and since you can't lie and tell her someone else told you, you'd get Gavin in trouble."

You might be correct. I will refrain from saying anything like that again in the future. But, I have not spoken to the young miss. I know nothing about her save she has picked up the piece sometime in the last day. Master Caelin, he said for me to leave her be and that he'd take care that she got here safely. I was so happy to hear from him after all this time. His mother, she would be so happy as well. Lewis asked him if Caelin had said anything about him. *Not yet, sir. He does not know who the miss is to be paired with. I will only talk to him when he speaks to me. He is afraid that someone will find out he lives.*

Lewis had an idea that everyone knew by now. It was still hard to wrap his mind around the fact that the dragon and the two men had been around longer than all his brothers combined. He thought of something else.

"His name is Caelin. What do you think we should do to keep you two straight?" The dragon said he'd decided to be called Warrior again. Just as his mistress had called him long ago. "I have another question. I mean, it's come up now that we're understanding a little more about our history than we did before. Why are we dragons and the queen, she only, the ruler of them?"

It is a good story, my lord. One that I will enjoy telling you. When the babe was born, the queen could have no one around her or the king, her husband, might find out. They were all loyal to her and only her, but the king, as you have guessed, was not a good man at all. He would have harmed them, killed who he needed to so that he could be well informed. Lewis said that made sense. *With her powerful magic, she turned me to a human for just a little while so that I might assist her in the birth of her son. It was for only a day. So during the last days of her breeding, she would change me into a human for a bit longer each time, only to return me to being a dragon.*

"She must have been extremely powerful." Warrior said that she was the greatest witch of all times. "So, what happened then?"

When the child was born, he was weak. I think it was because she was. I was afraid that the queen would die, and if she did, the child would be unsafe. As a human, I would not have been able to protect him as I needed. Had she died, I would have remained a human for all time, you see. Lewis stood to get himself a glass of

172

water as Warrior continued. *Just after his birth, the young king became ill, his frail body nearly not strong enough even to suckle. So I gave him a bit of me, some magic and blood. But it was only with the permission of his mother that I was able to help him, and thusly all of the McCade men after him.*

"Did you know that by doing so that you'd make his children dragons?" Warrior laughed. "I'm sorry, I don't understand."

I made him a dragon. He was weak, you see. My blood was enough to not just heal him, but to change him into something more. His mother, my queen, could also change into a dragon when she wished, but hers was with magic. Young Caelin, he could shift any time he wished because it was in his blood. Sometimes, it was at the oddest of times too. Lewis laughed when Warrior did, thinking of all the things that could go wrong with a child who knew not to be afraid of someone seeing him. *The staff did not know of him, as you know, so he and I, we'd go out into the fields far from the castle and I'd teach him to be the best dragon I could. His mother, she taught him the ways of her magic, how to use a sword and to hide.*

"He was as much a warrior as you were then." Warrior thanked him. "I guess that I should confess to my family what I've been up to. I don't think they're going to be upset, but I'm in need of their help on some things. Like…well, I almost hate to admit this, but I haven't any idea where to order wholesale food from. There are other things as well. Linen cleaning service. Staff and what they should wear. I've been so focused on the place that I completely forgot about the running of it."

I think you will be surprised at how much they know of what you are doing. He nodded. His mom knew, but she'd not betray him. However, each of them were an open book on anything should they only want to take a peek. *You're a good man, Lewis. Everyone that meets you, they know this as well.*

173

"I thank you, my friend, and you are a wonderful friend to me." As he began making a list of things he needed to discuss with his family, he thought of all the other things in his life that were going on. Too much, too many things going on at the moment to make him feel good. So, Lewis made him a list, several as it turned out, and concentrated on that one thing.

Several hours later—really, the only thing that had gotten him to look up from it was his belly growling over and over—Lewis thought he had a pretty good idea of what he was going to need. Even making the lists, not having any of it done, it made him feel better. Lewis liked lists.

Now all he had to do was find a time when they could all get together. Looking around, he knew what he had to do. It was time to christen Dragon's Lair. Pulling out his phone, he messaged everyone that they were to come to dinner at the Lair.

~~~

The alley between the two buildings was as clear as they could make it without raising suspicion about them being around. Vance looked over at Dalton, and wondered not for the first time if this was a good idea. Should he have taken the chance of doing this alone rather than bringing him in on it? He was sure that Dalton would be helpful, but he didn't want him to be hurt. Dalton was smart, good with a gun, and wouldn't take unnecessary chances like…well, like he would. Dalton was the best there was as far as he was concerned.

Stop overthinking this. He looked at Dalton again when he spoke. *You told me, like several hundred thousand times, what I'm to do, and I'll do it. I swear to you. It's a good plan. We're going to come out on top of this.*

This is not going to be like anything you've ever been on before. Dalton told him he was well aware of that. *You don't understand. You could be shot.*

174

You mean like you have been? Or perhaps knifed? Vance didn't like the fact that Dalton knew about his injuries. Nor that his wife had firsthand knowledge of a lot of other things. *Did I tell you that we heard from Jeff?*

I spoke to him. He had too, and now had knowledge that he was pretty sure would get them both killed. Especially Jeff. *For now, I'm putting this on the back burner. I need to get other things finished up before I can think of the men who have the trackers and figure out who they are. They're going to be paying for what they've done to me.*

It was a lie, and he was pretty sure that Dalton knew it was. Not only did he now know who had put them in his body, but the man who held them tracker too. A man that would be dead soon, he just wasn't aware of it yet. He moved closer to the window to see into the building before he let his mind wander too far down that path.

Vance could see the men working in the building. For three weeks now he'd been watching the ins and outs of the place enough to know their schedule. Delivery trucks were in on Saturday night. Sunday it was sorted. Monday through Wednesday they were stamped, and invoices were made out on Thursday. On Friday, today, they were boxed up, crated, and put on trucks to hit the stores that were paying less than half of the going rate for the shit.

As he made his way to the front of the building, leaving Dalton where he was, Vance assumed the role of one of the drivers. Just a few days ago he'd found one of them in a nearby hotel, and had taken not just his identification, but anything else that he had. The man, Howard Daniels, wouldn't be needing it anymore.

Startled out of his thoughts, he looked at the man who pointed a gun at him. Vance was armed as well, with more than just a gun, but he didn't draw on the man just yet. He

175

was waiting for the right time. And this wasn't it.

"Who the fuck are you?" He showed the man his ID, and stood still while he seemed to be looking it over for a test later. "Well, Daniels, you were to be here over two hours ago. You got you some pussy call or something?"

"No, I had shit to do." He rocked on his heels, wondering if this was going to be up before he began. "You want me to drive or not? I got a better gig if you don't."

The man pointed in the general directions of the trucks that were lined up against the back of the building. Vance made his way there now, looking to see if the same amount of guards were on duty as had been.

There are four men coming in. Two different limos, and a huge fucking truck. Looks to be armored. Like those suckers that come to pick up cash. Vance told him that was normal. *Normal? There is nothing normal about this, Vance.*

Okay, then it's normal for this shit. They both laughed, and Vance felt his tension roll away a little. *I'm going to have one of the trucks, once I leave this building, I'm going to make a left. You be at the corner, like we planned.*

Deal.

Vance started the truck up and tried to calm his heart. He was just letting out a long soft breath when someone pounded on the window. Rolling it down, he looked at the man there. He told him to get out.

I might be in trouble. Dalton said he was close. *Just don't get caught. When I get out of here, you might not want to be too close. I don't take prisoners when I'm in shit.*

Good to know. He got out of the truck when the man told him to. *Vance, you might be in more trouble than you think. There is some major shit going on out here. There are three...no, four cruisers coming in. Two of them aren't marked.*

Good guys or bad? Dalton said he didn't know just yet. *Stay safe, or Mom will kick our asses.*

Vance was afraid. Not for himself…he'd been at this too long to care if he lived or died. And now, it seemed, he couldn't die, but could be fucked up pretty bad. The man, no nametag to call him by, was looking over his identification again.

The thing was perfect. Better than he'd ever had made for him before when the government was involved. Vance had contacted Jeff, the gay nerd, as he called himself, a few hours after he'd gotten Daniels' information and told him he had something for him to do. It was to take the license that he'd gotten from Daniels reworked to be his. Jeff told him he wouldn't be caught for having a bogus license, and he'd make sure of it. The man handed it back to him without a word.

"Something up?" The man, Vance decided to call him Fats, said to shut the fuck up. Vance would, but only as long as it suited him. Dalton told him he was down to four men, not six. *You killing them off, little brother?*

Yes, they drew on me, so that makes it all fair in love and war. He laughed. *Down one more. These guys are really armed. I mean, some of this shit, I've never had the opportunity to see up close before. You should —*

When Dalton stopped talking, Vance felt something move over his body. He was sure it was his dragon, a beast that wasn't far from him, but he also knew that it would never come out. Not until he was unlucky enough to have a mate.

As he stood there waiting to be told what he was doing now, he looked around the big building. For all intents and purposes, from the outside it looked like it hadn't been touched in decades. But inside, it was state of the art.

Tables were lined up with several stamping areas. There were boxes of gloves to use for the people not only stamping there, but also carting them into boxes. Boxes he was sure had been stolen as well. They were marked just like the ones that legitimate stores would receive. The man in charge of this operation had gone to a great deal of expense to get this thing working. And the amount of money he was making made it all worthwhile.

Vance? I'm pretty sure that the person who is running this shit just got here. And you're not going to believe who it is. Vance asked him if it was the mayor. *Yes, I guess you would know that. But he's not alone. The governor is with him. Did you know that too?*

No, I had an idea it went further up the line, but not how far. Were they in one of the limos? Dalton told him separate. *Figures. Why share a ride and save gas and emissions when you can fuck up the world and steal too?*

The mic at the shoulder of the man holding him went off. It was difficult to understand, but from the look on the man's face, he'd bet he wasn't happy about it. Vance started to ask again what was going on, but the man turned and walked away. Vance got back in the truck and started it up. It was time to get the evidence that he needed.

I've got pictures, and the cameras we set up are running. Vance thanked his brother, glad now that he'd thought of it. *Also, the cops that came in, they're with the mayor. Protection, I guess. I've got some names to turn over, when and if they find someone to come in and take charge.*

I'm sure they think they have. In you. Vance smiled when his brother started cursing. *Yeah, you kiss your mate with that mouth?*

You can't seriously believe they're still thinking I'm going to take this job, do you? Vance said he would if he was them. *Not going to happen. I just don't have it in me anymore to do that.*

I don't blame you one bit. But as you can tell, they need someone to come in and take care of shit. He moved his truck forward

178

when he was waved out. *They're moving us. Be ready.*

This was the tricky part. He had to get out, his face and the truck information on camera. Then he had to be shown leaving the lot with all the goods, so that they'd not come back later and say that he'd gotten the truck with the contents from somewhere else. All good if you considered that he was willing to nearly lean out of the truck to do so, but he hadn't expected to have company when he did this. The mayor and governor showing up was a nice touch, but also made his job just a little more dangerous.

Camera is rolling on all of it.

He told Dalton that he was coming out now, but paused when he noticed that the governor was coming toward him. There were guards behind and in front of him, and Vance knew there was going to be trouble. As casually as he could, he reached into his boot and pulled out his gun. It was lying beside him when his door was pounded against once more.

"Vance? How the hell did you get in here?" He looked around. There wasn't any way that he knew who he was. "You are Vance McCade, aren't you? Heard tell you were looking to come in and try and make me look bad."

"I don't know what you're talking about." He got out and put his hands up when he was told. The gun at the back of his head was a little nerve wracking, but he complied. "I'm Howard Daniels. You must have me mistaken for —"

"I have a picture of you." He showed him the grainy yet very noticeable picture of him. "I heard that you were the best of the best. Probably a lie, I'm guessing. And not a very good one, if you ask me. But then, I'm not going to have to tell you that you're pretty much fucked with this one." Vance said nothing, trying to figure out who would have told that he was going to be there, and all he could come up with was the trackers in his body. "Here's what's going to happen now.

You're going to go with these fellows right here, and they're going to take care that you don't fuck with things that don't have shit to do with you. This money we're making? It's going to go to some pretty nice things."

"You are pretty well informed, Conrad. What do you suppose is going to happen when all this hits the paper?" Conrad Washington only laughed. "You think I'm kidding? Have a look to your right. You'll see a man with a camera pointed at you. Just behind you is a nice big van with listening equipment in it that's been recording for several weeks. What do you suppose they found?"

"You're lying. Not that it matters. You'll be long dead before any of this gets thrown out of court. I've had you thoroughly investigated, my man, and you are done. Do you really think I've just gotten into this line of work? How the hell do you suppose I financed all the pretty things I have?" Conrad laughed. "You just behave yourself, and I'll have these nice gentlemen do their job quickly."

"Come to me, babies." He wasn't sure it would work. Vance had no mate, but he was in trouble. He was an immortal, yes, but he didn't like pain any more than the next guy. So when the little dragons came to stand on either side of him, he put his hands down. "Conrad, I don't think you've done enough research on me. If you had, then you know that I never give up, nor do I lose."

The dragons moved as one. Vance was knocked back; he wasn't sure what had hit him, but his head exploded in pain just as he saw the small, hot flame. Smiling, he let the darkness take him.

CHAPTER 13

Gabe watched Vance. There was something so sad about him that her heart hurt for the man. She had a feeling that he was fighting demons, larger than his dragon could handle all the time. When he just sat there for several minutes, his food in front of him, for several minutes, she got up to go and sit beside him. He just stared at her, and she had a feeling that he really wasn't seeing her.

"Vance?" He nodded. "I'm here if you need me. I know that you think I can't handle whatever is going on in your head, but I want to help."

"She's coming." Gabe knew what he was referring too. Lewis had announced at dinner that he'd spoken to Warrior. "I have no idea what I'm supposed to do with her. Or how to…I can barely keep my head on straight. What will a female think of me?"

"She might surprise you." He laughed. It was bitter and cold. "You're running again, aren't you?"

"I have an assignment to do. You would understand that more than most, I think." She did. Gabe wasn't sure what she really knew, but in her heart, she knew that Vance was a man that did what was expected of him all the time. "I don't know when I'll be back. I can talk to the others, my brothers, keep tabs on them, but…. Your friend, Jeff, He's going to be able to

181

reach me quicker than anyone."

"He told me." He nodded as if he already knew that. "He's happy to be working for you. Jeff told me that you were a good man, dealt a shitty hand."

"He would know about that more than others, I think." They had met, Jeff had told her. Late one night after much back and forth, Jeff told her that he had let him know where he lived. "He's a good man. A smarter man than anyone that I've ever met."

"He said the same about you." Vance looked around the room, then back at her. She wanted him to tell her; whatever he was thinking, she wanted to know. Before she could ask, because she was sure he wasn't going to speak, he did.

"There is a man, one that I've known since I was a teenager, who is out to have me killed. He's fucked me over for the last time, and I need to take care of this before she comes here. Because I know, if he has any inkling that I might have someone in my life, he'll use her and kill her to get to me." Gabe asked him if he was going to go there now. "Not today. I have…these trackers are going to get me killed if I do. I know that you're aware of that, but you have no idea who this man is, what kind of things he controls."

"I can help you." He shook his head. It was perhaps the saddest thing she'd ever seen. "I can help you, Vance. I want to."

"At what risk? There are risks. More than even you can imagine, and I have a feeling that you can see more than most. You can, can't you?" She asked him if he meant something magical. "No, I just mean with people. You have this gift, I think. One that lets you see not just the person, but everything about them. Pain. Hurt. Even when they're terrified out of their mind about something."

"I don't know. Perhaps." He nodded and looked at the

door. "Don't go, Vance. We can help you if you let us."

"I know that. And I believe it too. Believe that my family, you and the other wives included, would do everything in your power to help me. But I'm afraid that I have to fight this one on my own."

Gabe told him that she understood. And when he stood up, she did as well. "At least let them know this time. Don't just disappear in the middle of the night."

He looked around the pretty restaurant, the one that Lewis had worked very hard to get finished, and then at her. She loved this man. Perhaps more than she did the others, excluding Dalton. And when he opened his arms to hug her, she went right to him.

"Don't change. I love you, Gabe." Tears fought and won as they spilled down her cheeks. "When she gets here, I'll be back. Until then, I have to plan and make sure that she'll be safe with me."

"I understand." He kissed the top of her head and moved back. It was the hardest thing she'd ever done, letting him go. Then he left her standing there.

"He'll be all right." Gabe leaned back against Dalton when he came up behind her. "He will be all right. More than any of the rest of us might be."

"Vance said he was going to make his mate was safe. I wonder...do you suppose he means to take care of this thing with the trackers now?" Dalton said he'd wait for a little while. "Why is that? I mean, I think he knows who it is."

"He does, but timing is everything." She wasn't sure what that meant and asked him. "If he goes in too soon, things would go badly for a great many people. I don't know why I think that, but I do. Also, and this is the most important thing, he needs to make sure that he isn't bringing things down on top of us. He feels, and probably rightly so, that the thing with

183

the warehouse was wrong."

The dragons had destroyed everything. Not just the building, but the men and the trucks as well. The place looked like a bomb had gone off there, and Gabe shivered when she thought of the amount of heat that had been used to do that.

"The governor was found dead there. Do you think that ended it? I mean, for this town." He told her he thought it would make someone think twice before coming here again. "Once this hits the paper, with the evidence found on the mayor and him, things will never be the same around here."

"No, a lot of people will be brought to justice by this. A lot of people were receiving those stolen goods. It's not going to go well for them once the Feds step in." She knew there were several in town, all of them asking questions no one was answering. Especially not them. "The dragons, they saved us a lot of time, but they did a great deal of damage as well."

The warehouse and the buildings on either side of it were destroyed. The one that she'd been held in, the building where she'd been taken, was gone as well. She wondered if Lyna had done that, made sure that it wasn't there as a reminder to her. Turning in Dalton's arms, she asked him how he liked the restaurant.

"Unbelievable, isn't it? I mean, this was what Lewis dreamed of his entire life. And now he has it." Gabe had given him a list of names for wholesalers after talking to Jeff. He had an insider look on just about anything. The pack was going to set up a list of potential employees, ones to come in and help with the cooking, as well as to wait tables. Aisha had given him a working list of what sort of things she'd do to improve the overall look of the place. Mostly it was small things, but Gabe thought them to be great ideas.

"He's going to be a success." Dalton said he thought so as well. "I cannot wait to see who his mate is. I'm betting she'll have him whipped into making a profit the first day she's here."

"I hope you're right, I just hope that she's as loving to him as he needs. Lewis is extremely insecure." Gabe thought that all the McCade men were, but said nothing. "I love you, Gabe. I think we should get married."

"I agree. How about tomorrow? Here?" He laughed and said that Lewis might need more time than that. "Oh, I don't know. I bet he could pull off about anything right now."

They were still laughing about it as they made their way home. Gabe wondered, not for the first time tonight, if the new mate was safe. And if Caelin was helping this woman like he had her. She'd bet that he was, but also thought she'd not be as easygoing as Lewis was. They were going to be a pair.

~~~

Caelin sat and watched the woman. She was a beautiful person, but sad. He had been watching over her family and her kind for many centuries, just waiting for this child to be born. And now that she was here, his watching had turned to so much more. When she sat beside him, not asking for permission at all, he had to smile, but inwardly. She was touchy about such things.

"I don't like you." He nodded. Raven had said this to him many times since he'd approached her about the brooch. "You told me when I took it that it would lead me down a merry path. I thought it would be a merry one, not one filled with trouble."

"All life gives you trouble, young Raven. It is not my fault that you didn't ask more questions at the time." She snorted at him, a habit that she'd picked up from her mother, no doubt. "What bothers you more? The fact that I was right, or that you had fun while doing this thing I asked of you?"

185

"Both, but I didn't care for what I had to do to get it for you. His magic, black as the coal that heats my home, will destroy a great many people before this is done." Caelin agreed. "This man, the one you said I was set for, does he have any idea what is coming to him? What sort of magic, white and black, will be his for the taking?"

"I have told you, I cannot give you information that will change your future. I could have gone to you both, ended this before it began, really. But it has to play out the way it plays. I have only…I think you called it tweaked, a few things to make sure that the children were not harmed." She nodded and looked around her yard without seeing it. "You have done well here, Raven. It will only get better as time goes on."

"My mother and father are buried here. My sisters too. All generations of my family are right here on this land, land that you told me would be helpful in my studies. It'll be hard to leave them behind." He nodded, his own heart painfully full for the same reasons. To lose someone that filled your heart while alive hurt more than anything, he thought. "This man, he'd better be a good one, or I shall hunt you down and end your life."

"Not a threat I take lightly, Raven, but I assure you, he is the best there is, and he will care for you like none other." Nodding, she leaned her head back and let the sun shine on it. "I could heal you."

"Nay, you cannot. I suppose you could, but at what cost to you? You told me, long ago, that my lack of sight was what made me powerful. Do not take that from me now when things are coming so close to the end." He nodded. "I will go to the family soon. Not to meet them, but to feel them. You'll go as well?"

"No, I cannot. I have things to do. Another bride to keep safe." She nodded again and said nothing. Asked none of the questions that he was sure were circling around in her head. "When this is done, you'll be happy, Raven. I promise."

"Do not make promises that you cannot keep, my lord." He nodded, then told her he was sorry. "Your sire, he is around. I can feel him. His blackness is as much a beacon to me as your scent is. He will try his best to kill the two of us when he finds out what we've done."

Caelin had worked hard for this moment in time. His father lived still not because of the magic he thought he had, but because it was important to the family, all McCades from now to all time, to have him here. His father, his sire, played a great part in this. Sadly, Caelin didn't know what it might be just yet.

"No other family has gotten this far before." Caelin told her that he was aware of that. "I'm afraid. Not of the coming together of them all, that will be wonderfully beautiful, but that I might be the one that fails them."

"I don't know how you think that to come to pass. You have been prepared for this for the whole of your life." She told him that was the point. "You will do us all well, Raven. There is no worry from me on that."

When they parted ways, her going to her little house that sat in the mountain, him to his place in the town that his children's children lived in, he sat on the rocking chair that had been in the castle when he'd been but a child. There was still much to do, many things that could go wrong, but he wasn't as worried about that as he was the young woman he'd just left.

Her blindness was what she'd suffered when she helped his father attain his magic. Her sight having been forfeited when she had agreed to help. Caelin's father had treated her poorly and had nearly killed her. When Raven came to Caelin with a plea to bring him down, Caelin decided to return her sight when all was completed. To her, it had been a small price to pay. To Caelin, it had been too much, but it was done now, and he would repair her when the time came.

Caelin hadn't foreseen that some things—not all, but some things—were hard for him to see. His mother had given him this gift, the ability to see into the future, when he'd been but a child. Her warrior, he'd given him gifts as well. The dragon in them all was only the single thing that Warrior knew about.

Putting out his hand, he called for the dragon that was on his body. She pulled from his fingertips and sat very still on his palm. The blueness of her defied description. The strength that she had belied the smallness of her. She was, Caelin was sure, the strongest dragon of all time.

"They will need you soon." She nodded, bowing her head low. "Go to the female now and keep her safe. She knows of the jewel, but has yet to touch it. I wish for you to keep her safe for them."

I shall, my lord. When she didn't move, he waited. There was much she could ask him, but only a few things he had answers for. *I can feel him. His magic is stronger than it was just a fortnight ago.*

"Yes, he's getting stronger. But it will do him little good when the time comes." She looked at him, questions aplenty on her face. "I will take care that he is where he needs to be, my lovely. Then when he is gone, you will rise again."

I have missed you. He nodded, his heart full for the pain of missing her as well. *When this is done, what will happen to you, my lord? To me?*

"I know not, and you know that as well." She nodded. "I hope we can live with them, enjoy them close up. But I cannot look to my own future."

I shall go now then. Protect her with my life. He nodded, knowing that she'd do that without her confirming it. *My lord? When you have the pieces together, do you think your mother, the queen, will come?*

"I have not seen her." He had, and he was pretty sure that the little dragon knew that. "Go now, before I beg you for a game of chess and lose to you."

Caelin rocked back and forth, clearing his mind of all thoughts save the man who had planted the seed that made him. His father was going to die, but he had a destiny to complete first. Putting out his hand again, the sword of his family appeared. He'd have to make sure that it was in the hands of the right person before too much longer. The magic of it, which no one knew about, would be the only thing that would bring the family to a whole. The magic of the McCades.

"Go to him." The sword hummed its magic at him. "You will know the time to show what you are to him. Until then, I need for you to make him safe as well."

After the sword left him, Caelin went into his home. It was nothing like the façade that it appeared to be from the outside, but the grandest castle ever built. He was both excited and nervous to know that soon Grady and his bride would be there to awaken the magic within. Caelin smiled.

"So much going on and nothing complete. Soon. But for now, I must watch and wait." He reached for Warrior to make sure that he was doing as he asked him to do. Wait as well. Things were soon going to come to a head, and everyone had to be patient.

"Soon, my children. Soon." Caelin went to the room where he'd last seen his mother. He lay upon the cold stone, thinking about her. And when the tears that fell for her and only her hit the cold stone, he wrote her name there, as he did every night. "I love you, my mother. More than I could ever show you."

Caelin slept there, the stone warming under him so that

he'd not be chilled. Thanking the castle for its protection, Caelin slept. It was draining to him to have so much of himself spread around, but in the end, he knew this was going to be worth it. Or so he hoped.

Before You Go...

HELP AN AUTHOR

write a review

THANK YOU!

Share your voice and help guide other readers to these wonderful books. Even if it's only a line or two your reviews help readers discover the author's books so they can continue creating stories that you'll love. Login to your favorite retailer and leave a review. Thank you.

AWARD WINNING, BESTSELLING AUTHOR

Kathi Barton, winner of the Pinnacle Book Achievement award as well as a best-selling author on Amazon and All Romance books, lives in Nashport, Ohio with her husband Paul. When not creating new worlds and romance, Kathi and her husband enjoy camping and going to auctions. She can also be seen at county fairs with her husband who is an artist and potter.

Her muse, a cross between Jimmy Stewart and Hugh Jackman, brings her stories to life for her readers in a way that has them coming back time and again for more. Her favorite genre is paranormal romance with a great deal of spice. You can visit Kathi online and drop her an email if you'd like. She loves hearing from her fans. aaronskiss@gmail.com.

Follow Kathi on her blog: http://kathisbartonauthor. blogspot.com/

www.ingramcontent.com/pod-product-compliance
Lightning Source LLC
Chambersburg PA
CBHW032138170626

46808CB00006B/2283